by

Michael R. Martin

Acknowledgements

Special thanks go to:

The MTG Collective (Mike, Chris, Sue and Jack) for their no-nonsense critique.

Christine Johnson (who writes as C J Harter) for a thoroughly professional edit.

Captain Graham Martlew, of HG Helicopters Scotland Ltd, for his technical advice. Any inaccuracies, regarding helicopter flight, are down to me.

Alex Naylor and all the staff at the King's Head Hotel for making the location research so enjoyable despite the wind and rain.

Celestial Raven for permission to include her photograph in the back cover artwork.

My parents for their belief and support.

Last, but by no means least, my partner, Lez, for her continued patience and things too numerous to mention here.

About the Author

Mike Martin has a degree in mechanical engineering and a HND in multimedia.

He has worked as a design engineer, a volunteer IT tutor, a medical records officer and is currently a freelance graphic designer and computer animator.

He is the author of SCREAMS IN THE WOODS.

He lives near Wigan.

AREA 62

"Only the small secrets need to be protected.
The big ones are kept secret by public incredulity."

Marshall McLuhan

Prologue

Route 93, Nevada, USA

Tuesday, 4th September, 1973

Bill Klein got out of the hire car and surveyed the derelict gas stop. It was hard to say how long it'd been left to the mercy of the sharp dust and searing Mojave heat; nothing looked new for long out here.

A row of spent gas pumps pointed to the long prefab diner.

His heart picked up pace as he walked across the cracked forecourt.

He'd heard stories of bodies buried out here: mob hits tucked away in shallow graves under the rocks and Joshua trees. If this *was* a set-up, he'd come too far to back out.

Sweat beaded his forehead and trickled between his shoulder blades.

Under the tattered awnings, Venetian blinds sagged haphazardly behind the garish script of cut price menus.

He pushed the shattered doors and peered inside.

Rays of sunlight stabbed the musty interior, but the hulking steel counter and tall bar stools remained in shadow. A figure in silhouette sat at a booth in the far corner.

As he approached, the man stood up and gestured at the opposite seat.

'We don't have long,' he said. 'I suggest you take out your notebook.'

Klein sat down and reached into his jacket.

The man leaned forward. 'I'll tell you everything I know, but you must keep an open mind – most of what you're about to hear is insane.'

Klein clicked his ballpoint. 'Ready when you are.'

Part One

The Sitting Tenant

Chapter One

Cranshaw, England

Thursday, 6th March, 2014

Colin Thurcroft mopped the steamy window with a paper napkin and watched another taxi glide to a halt at the rank down the street. He checked his watch for the third time in as many minutes and sipped his coffee. There were only three other customers in the New Moon Café, and the scruffy, pencil-thin man in the knitted beanie had smiled at him once too often. Colin felt obliged to return the gestures, but he was treading a fine line between encouragement and politeness.

The electronic door chime interrupted another awkward grin.

A man in a blue suit under a beige raincoat entered and strode towards him. 'Morning, Mr Thurcroft. Sorry I'm a tad late, but town hall powwows often overrun.'

They shook briefly. 'Hello, Mr Dewhurst.'

Dewhurst squeezed his ample frame into the opposite chair. His curly, grey hair appeared more unruly than usual and biscuit crumbs peppered his bushy beard.

Colin lifted his mug. 'Can I get you a drink?'

'No, I'd better not.'

Colin glanced through the window. 'I've been keeping watch for council vehicles.'

Dewhurst squinted at the wall clock. 'If they're not here by ten past, I'll make a call.'

'Thanks again for this,' Colin said. 'I really appreciate everything you've done.'

'Not at all. We'd rather taken our eye off the ball with that particular property. Your enthusiasm gave us a deserved kick up the backside.'

'I knew it was right the first time I saw it.'

'Hiking gear will be a welcome change from pound shops and coffee bars. Shame you're not closer to the town centre, but it's a start.'

'That's how I see it. There's an untapped market here: four national parks are only an hour away.'

'How long did you say you've been trading?'

'I started online eight years ago, but this will be my first retail outlet.'

'At the end of the day, you can't beat trying something on.'

'We do have a clear-cut returns policy if items don't fit, but I wouldn't disagree.'

'I often browse the internet; however, when it comes to … '

Colin turned to follow his gaze.

A white panel van, displaying the borough coat of arms, was reversing into a spot directly opposite the café.

'The eagle has landed.' Dewhurst got to his feet. 'I shan't be a minute, Mr Thurcroft.'

Colin drained his cup and wiped the window again.

Dewhurst approached the van, and a man in a bright yellow tabard lowered the driver's window and leaned out. After a brief conversation, the van drove off, and Dewhurst returned to the café.

'Think I'll have that drink after all.' He tapped Colin's mug. 'Can I get you a refill?'

'Problem?'

'We wanted to get in there with the minimum of fuss. Since the fire escape is in such a precarious state, the plan was to go through a second floor window and unbolt the front door from the inside, but it seems my Health and Safety guru isn't happy.'

'So what happens now?'

'I've instructed them to remove the boards and break the door.'

Colin grabbed his mug. 'In that case, I'll have another coffee.'

Chapter Two

Dewhurst stirred his tea. 'I'll bring you up to speed while we're waiting.' He took a cautious sip. 'As you are aware from my recent letter, the owner's solicitors are no longer in a position to oppose the compulsory purchase.'

Colin nodded. 'Did you find out why?'

'Apparently, the sizeable fund Mr Manning set aside to fight his corner is exhausted. What's more, he hasn't had any contact with them for nearly eight years, and all efforts to trace him have come to naught.'

'So he's legally dead?'

'That's our understanding, but I need to acquaint you with a recent development.'

'Go on.'

'His sole remaining sibling has been located and made aware of the situation.'

Colin sighed. 'There's always a catch.'

'Quite the opposite: she wants a quick sale, and her solicitor has sanctioned our plan to access the property and evaluate its condition. At her time of life, I don't suppose I'd have the vim for legal wrangles.'

'So what happens now?'

'We need to do a full structural survey and make an offer to her. If she accepts, we'll clear the contents, make good any pressing repairs and put the property up for sale.'

'Hold on, I thought I had first refusal?'

'You do, but I'll need a verbal decision today and a written one within a week.'

'What's the rush?'

'Let's just say the ball's rolling, and my hands are tied.'

'The bank's agreed the loan in principle, but I'll need time to sort out an independent surveyor's report.'

'If you're up against it, I *might* be able to pull a few strings.'

Colin frowned. 'Thanks … '

'I'll do what I can to – '

A mobile phone rang.

Dewhurst reached into his coat pocket. 'Excuse me, Mr Thurcroft.' He glanced at the screen and held it to his ear. 'Hello ... '

Colin watched his forehead furrow.

'Don't go any further; I'll be there in a jiffy.' He ended the call and grimaced. 'I've got a feeling it's going to be one of those days.'

'What's happened?'

'They've got through the front door, but it's boarded up from the inside as well.'

Colin followed Dewhurst across the road and into the side street. Fifty yards down, the council van was parked with the rear doors open. The driver and a much younger man, both dressed in yellow tabards and hardhats, were throwing broken boards into the back.

The three-storey, Victorian building divided two narrow streets. The windows on the first two floors hid behind a collage of rotten wood and corrugated steel splashed with torn posters and hurried graffiti. Sagging gutters teamed with grass and weeds, and grimy paint peeled from the sandstone lintels and the ornate arch above the door. Yet, even in such an egregious state of neglect, it appeared sturdier and altogether more imposing than its much younger, utilitarian neighbours;

almost as if it had wandered away from its siblings in the high street and got stuck there, hemmed in by a rigid embrace of drab brick walls and soulless windows.

The heavy, panelled door had been removed to reveal a neat row of pale planks.

Dewhurst stooped to peer through a gap.

'I wouldn't bother,' the driver said. 'We couldn't see jack shit with a torch.'

Dewhurst turned around. 'We need to check the back door.'

'We'd have to force the yard gates to get at it.'

'Couldn't young Zak here climb over?'

'And cut himself to ribbons on rusty spikes and broken glass?'

'Sorry,' Colin said. 'But why can't we just remove the planks?'

'I'm afraid it's not that straightforward,' Dewhurst said. 'Someone has secured the property from the inside, which suggests they might still be in there.'

'Seriously?' Colin said. 'It's been boarded up for *forty* years.'

'I wasn't referring to the original owner.'

'He means squatters,' the driver said.

'Shit,' Colin said under his breath.

Dewhurst pursed his lips and studied the door. 'Gareth, how would you feel about removing just one of those planks?

'You're the boss.'

'If I can reach in with the torch, I'll have a better idea of what we're up against.'

Gareth handed a long Maglite to Dewhurst, and then went to work with a crowbar. Colin jumped when the plank cracked, leaving a dark gap like a missing tooth.

Gareth stepped back, and Dewhurst eased the torch inside.

After what seemed like an age, he withdrew his arm and wiped the wood splinters from his sleeve. 'Remarkable.'

'What's the score?' Gareth said.

'As far as I can see, there's nothing out of place. Even the shelves are fully stocked.'

Colin ran his fingers through his hair. 'Thank Christ for that.'

Gareth thumped Zak's arm. 'Get the big lamp and a couple more hardhats.'

Colin was the last to step through the doorway.

The fusty ground floor was a maze of wooden shelves crammed with toys and games devoid of microchips and clever software. A veil of fine dust and limp cobwebs clung to every surface, but the colourful packaging was still clear.

Gareth's torch picked out a wide stair case in the middle of the shop.

'Wait here,' he said to Dewhurst. 'We'll check the next floor.'

He ascended in measured steps with the crowbar swaying at his side. Zak hesitated for a moment before following him into the gloom.

Dewhurst went to the bottom of the stairs and raised the lamp.

Colin perused an aisle until a particular box caught his attention.

He picked it up and blew the dust away.

A shiny motorcycle, ridden by a man in Stars and Stripes leathers and helmet, leapt towards him; in the background, a bold, equally patriotic number one declared *Evel Knievel* to be the *King of The Stuntmen*. It took him back to a distant Christmas Day and family cats terrorised by a wind-up toy.

His recollections took flight when Gareth reappeared on the stairs.

'First floor's full of bikes,' he said. 'We're going up top now.'

Colin returned the box and followed Dewhurst up the stairs.

Serried ranks of dusty saddles and pitted chrome reached into the darkness.

Dewhurst placed the lamp on the carved newel post and walked towards a row of bicycles with high riser handlebars. He pulled a sky blue one from its stand and brushed the dust from the long padded saddle. 'I used to have one just like this.'

Colin joined him. 'Bit before my time, but I know a Raleigh Chopper when I see one.'

Dewhurst squeezed a creaky brake lever. 'What bicycle did you ride in your youth?'

Shouts from above stifled his response.

Chapter Three

Colin strode towards the door marked *Private* and pulled it open. A narrow staircase climbed towards a faint glow of natural light.

'Hello!' he shouted. 'You okay up there?'

There was no reply.

His shadow swept upstairs when Dewhurst approached with the lamp.

Colin cupped his mouth. 'Gareth! Zak!'

Silence.

Dewhurst sighed. 'I've got a bad feeling about this.'

Colin began to climb the stairs.

'That's probably not a good idea,' Dewhurst said.

'Any better ones?'

Dewhurst followed a few steps behind. 'Please don't do anything rash.'

At the top, a frosted glass door opened onto a carpeted hallway. The sound of retching reached them from an open door on the opposite side.

Colin crossed the hallway and peered into the room.

Zak was bent over the kitchen sink with Gareth's hand on his back.

'What happened?' Colin said.

Gareth turned around and winked. 'Just lost his cherry. First one's always the worst.'

'Damn and blast!' Dewhurst said. 'Where is it?'

'Next room along.'

'Recent?'

Gareth shook his head. 'Anything but. Looks like a sudden death, but the weird hat is a new one on me.'

'Weird hat?' Dewhurst said. 'What sort of weird hat?'

Gareth grinned. 'Why don't you look for yourself?'

He glared at Gareth and pulled out his phone. 'Today just gets better and better.'

Colin sidestepped him and went towards the next door.

He hesitated for a moment, and then pushed it open.

A wash of grey light from the lank net curtains revealed a room furnished entirely in early twentieth century. A leather armchair had its back to the door with what looked like a hairy coconut in an upended wicker bowl on the head rest.

He walked into the room, took a deep breath and turned towards it.

Jesus H!

He stepped back and banged into a bureau.

The mummified, male body sat upright with its bony fingers clutching the arms of the chair. The lower jaw had slumped onto the chest to reveal an arc of neat white teeth and dark fillings. A greasy, brown substance caked the lower half of a patterned shirt and the flared jeans down to the knees; it had spilled over the front of the chair and pooled on the carpet.

It was the most gruesome thing he'd ever seen.

He wanted to turn away, but his eyes were drawn to the strange contraption on the corpse's head. It consisted of around twenty small black disks mounted in a crude wooden frame held together by screws and insulation tape. An untidy web of fine wires reached out from each disk to a small circuit board on the back.

'You've met Davros then?' Gareth said from the doorway.

A clear image of the science fiction villain flashed into Colin's mind. He tried not to smile, but the similarity was striking.

'What *is* that on his head?'

Gareth shrugged. 'Your guess is as good as mine, mate.'

'Do you think it killed him?'

Gareth pointed at the circuit board. 'Not with a nine volt battery.'

Colin glanced around the room. 'The décor's a bit weird, isn't it?'

'Just a bit. And there's a couple more like this – old fashioned, but not as old as this.'

'Where's Dewhurst?'

'In the kitchen. He won't show his face in here.'

'And Zak?'

'Shaking like a shitting dog.'

Chapter Four

Colin stepped through the front door and took a few deep breaths.

A police car crawled up the cobbled street at the side of the shop and stopped.

Two officers, a young woman and a middle-aged man, got out and walked over.

'Morning,' she said brightly. 'Mr Dewhurst?'

'No, he's still in there,' Colin said. 'Top floor.'

She peered through the door, and then eased a small torch from her belt.

When they were both inside, he pulled out his phone and tapped the screen.

His wife answered almost immediately.

'How did it go?'

'Okay, Jan, apart from the sitting tenant.'

'You're joking?'

'I wish I was, but, don't worry, he won't be hanging around.'

'How do you mean?'

'Poor bugger's been brown bread for Christ knows how long.'

'Oh, God! Where did you find him?'

'In an armchair on the top floor.'

'Is it the owner?'

'Most likely, but we'll have to wait and see.'

'Are you still going ahead?'

'I think so, but we'll rearrange a proper look around when the police have finished doing whatever they have to do.'

'What will you do for the rest of the day?'

'I'm going back to the office, but I might skip lunch.'

'Can't say I blame you.'

'There's a lot more to tell, but I'll save it 'til tonight, yeah?'

'Okay, Col, but phone me if you want to talk.'

'I will. Bye, love.'

'Bye.'

He dropped the phone into his pocket and headed off to the multi-storey car park.

In a shuttered doorway, a few yards from the main road, a tall, grey-haired man flicked away a burning cigarette. He strode towards the shop and stopped for a moment to glance at the top floor and make the sign of the cross.

Chapter Five

Tuesday, 11th March

Jan Thurcroft reached across the arm of the sofa and handed the buzzing phone to Colin.

'Hello, Mr Dewhurst.'

'Good evening, Mr Thurcroft. I'm sorry to bother you at this hour, but I thought you'd want to know that the police have finished with the shop, and I can arrange a proper viewing tomorrow if convenient.'

'Err … yeah. What time did you have in mind?'

'I've got the surveyor there in the morning, so how about two o'clock?'

'Two's fine, and I'd appreciate a heads up on what he finds.'

'No problem at all. I suggest we meet in the café as before.'

'The café's good for me.'

'I'll see you there then.'

'Just one more thing,' Colin said. 'Have the police identified the body?'

'The advanced decomposition has compromised the autopsy, but it *is* Eric Manning, and there's no observable evidence of foul play.'

'What about the weird hat?'

'It wasn't mentioned.'

'Do they know how long he's been dead?'

'Thirty years or more.'

'But didn't you say his solicitor last heard from him eight years ago?'

'Ah … yes … unfortunately, I'm not at liberty to discuss that.'

'As a potential buyer, I think I should have *all* the facts.'

'I can see your point, but the police inspector advised discretion.'

'Then give me his name, and I'll ask him myself.'

'That won't be necessary, but please keep this strictly between us.'

'Of course.'

'There *is* a significant discrepancy between the time of death and his last contact with his solicitor. They found his official documents in a metal tin, but his birth certificate and bank books weren't there. That's all I know at present, but I'll keep you abreast of any developments.'

'Sounds like somebody wanted us to think he was still alive.'

'It would seem so.'

'I can understand stealing his identity to empty his bank account, but why pay a solicitor to fight the compulsory purchase?'

'It's most puzzling, but some fraudsters will go to any length to cover their tracks. I suspect the shop was broken into post mortem, and, with the death evidently unreported, they must've realised they were onto a good thing.'

'Did you notice any signs of forced entry?'

'I can't say I did, but I was somewhat preoccupied.'

'You and me both.'

'I trust it hasn't put you off.'

Colin smiled. 'I'll see you tomorrow, Mr Dewhurst.'

'Goodnight then.'

'Goodnight.'

He put the phone on the arm of the chair and sighed.

'The plot thickens,' Jan said.

'Indeed … I thought it was too good to be true when I first set eyes on it.'

'What're you going to do?'

He grabbed the TV Magazine. 'Make him an offer he *might* refuse.'

Wednesday, 12th March

Colin adjusted his hardhat and leaned across the kitchen sink. 'Something's not right.'

'Specifically?' Dewhurst said.

'The fire doors are secure and none of the top floor windows have been forced.'

'Not sure I follow.'

'Nobody's been in here since Eric Manning died unless they had keys … '

'I think we should leave that to the police, don't you?'

Colin frowned. 'Which means he probably knew the person who stole his identity.'

Dewhurst glanced at his watch. 'Time is pressing, Mr Thurcroft – the rear yard is next on the agenda.'

Colin chewed his lip and surveyed the room.

'Mr Thurcroft?'

He turned to Dewhurst and smiled. 'Sorry, I was miles away.'

Dewhurst led the way down to the ground floor, where he lumbered through the cramped stockroom to a door in the corner. He held it open and beckoned Colin through.

The rear yard was larger than expected. A dishevelled line of rotten wooden boxes and rusty dustbins backed against the far wall. Murky puddles and clumps of vibrant weeds crowded the rumpled jigsaw of concrete flags. Wind-blown litter hugged every corner.

Dewhurst brushed some dust from his jacket and gestured at the dirt-streaked double gates. 'And there's delivery access from Endell Street.'

Colin kicked a crumpled Styrofoam cup against the wall and surveyed the jagged line of broken glass along the top. 'Bit keen on security, wasn't he?'

'That will all have to go,' Dewhurst said. 'It's illegal now.'

Colin's gaze travelled up the back of the shop to the twisted TV aerial on the broad chimney stack. 'Could you drop the price if I take it sold as seen?'

Dewhurst cleared his throat. 'In principle.'

'Is that a *yes* or a *no*?'

'A lower price will affect our offer to Mr Manning's sister.'

'But you're saving money if I do the repairs.'

'How much were you thinking of?'

Colin smiled and rubbed his chin.

Chapter Six

Monday, 24th March

Colin looked up from his laptop when Alan Sharrock, his distribution manager of some six years, rapped on the door and strode into his office. 'Kath said you wanted a word.'

'Good news, Alan.'

'Go on, make my day.'

Colin glanced at his watch. 'Just over an hour ago, I became a shop keeper.'

'You mean the bank let you put your name on the deeds.'

'Exactly.'

'Right then, I'd better get my head around the stock list.'

'I'd hang fire if I were you.'

'Why?'

'I negotiated a lower price for sold as seen, which means there's a lot more to do before we even think about getting product in there.'

'Structural?'

'The roof's in a bad way but repairable, there's rising damp on the ground floor, all the windows and gutters are shagged, the wiring's been condemned and the fire escape's a write off. Apart from that, it's in tip-top condition.'

Alan grinned. 'Hope it's worth it, Col.'

'It will be.'

'What about the stock that's in there?'

'I'll get you a set of keys tomorrow. Let me know what's worth selling and what's for the skip.'

Alan nodded. 'What're you planning to do with all that furniture on the top floor?'

'Good question.'

'I'd get it valued, Col, some of it might be worth a bob or two.'

'It might, but I'm not ready to get rid until I've done a bit more digging.'

Alan shook his head. 'Here we go again.'

'There *has* to be a link between his weird hat, the odd décor and the identity theft.'

'Like what?'

'I haven't a clue, but I might know more this afternoon.'

'How come?'

'I'm going to see his sister.'

'Tell me you're joking.'

'Dewhurst let slip she's in that new retirement home on Horsham Road.'

'And what if she tells you to piss off?'

'I've already phoned her and arranged it.'

'Does Jan know about this?'

'Not yet.'

Alan rolled his eyes and sighed.

Colin winked. 'Nothing ventured, nothing gained.'

Derwent Court stood where, thirty years before, an engineering company had employed a third of the town's workforce. A central, gabled tower linked two flat roof blocks enfolded by four tiers of balconied windows framed in pinkish brick and yellow stone. It exuded an air of cheerful modernity and stuck out like a sore thumb on a road of sombre Edwardian town houses and a derelict pub.

Colin drove through the wrought iron gates and parked his black Alfa Romeo Giulietta in the visitor car park.

Inside the steel framed vestibule, a bald, thickset man in a shirt and tie was studying a large monitor. He looked up as Colin approached and smiled.

'Good afternoon,' he said. 'How can I help you?'

'I phoned this morning,' Colin said. 'Joyce Manning is expecting me.'

'What name is it?'

'Thurcroft – Colin Thurcroft.'

The man tapped the keyboard and adjusted the thin microphone attached to his ear.

'Hello, Mrs Manning, I have a visitor for you.' He glanced at Colin. 'Yes, it is – righto then, I'll send him up.'

He gestured at the solid double doors. 'Second floor, apartment twenty-three.'

Colin thanked him and went through.

He decided against the lift and headed for the stairs.

Each floor was a wash of pastel walls punctuated by vapid abstract paintings and the occasional potted plant.

At apartment twenty-three, he pressed the green button on the plastic intercom.

After a few moments, the speaker crackled into life.

'Hello?'

'Hello, Mrs Manning, it's Colin Thurcroft.'

The door opened to reveal a petite, elderly lady in a white blouse and long black skirt. Frizzy grey hair reached to her hunched shoulders and a warm smile revealed a neat line of false teeth.

'Do come in, Mr Thurcroft.'

'Just Colin, please.'

The bland colour scheme extended into a hallway infused by the faint aroma of lavender and stale urine.

'Then you must call me Joyce.' She closed the door. 'Go through to the lounge and make yourself comfortable.'

The spacious room contained a variety of elegant, antique furniture somewhat at odds with the insipid green walls and beige carpet.

Colin sat down on the small leather sofa, facing the flame effect gas fire.

Joyce shuffled into the room. 'Would you like something to drink?'

'No thanks, Mrs Man – sorry, Joyce.'

'Let me know if you change your mind; it's no trouble.' She lowered herself into the armchair and smiled. 'So, you've bought the shop?'

'Yes, I have. The paperwork was completed this morning.'

'And you want to know about my brother?'

He nodded.

'Are you aware we hadn't spoken for forty years?'

'I gathered as much, but I didn't know who else to talk to.'

'Did *you* find his body?'

'No, it was one of the council workmen.'

'It's so sad to think of him sitting there year after year. All those people going about their business in the streets below. And me, getting on with my life, hardly giving him a second thought.'

'I imagine he just fell asleep and never woke up.'

'I'd like to think so, but, according to the police, he died not too long after closing the shop, so he'd still have been a relatively young man.'

'How old was he when you last saw him?'

'Let me think now … thirty five or six and in good health.'

'Hmm, I see what you mean … '

'And it seems somebody's been pretending to be him.'

'Really?' Colin said with feigned surprise.

'A person, claiming to be Eric, was in contact with his solicitors until relatively recently. They were under instruction to stop the council getting their hands on the shop.'

'Can you think of anybody who would profit from this?'

She shook her head. 'The police asked the same question.'

'I'm sure they'll get to the bottom of it.'

'I wouldn't hold your breath.'

Chapter Eight

Colin shifted in his seat. 'Do you mind if I ask a straight question?'

Joyce smiled. 'Not at all.'

'Why didn't you oppose the compulsory purchase?'

'A legal dispute at my time of life? No, thank you. And what do I want with a dilapidated building that my brother died in?'

'Surely you could've sold it?'

'I'm quite content with the council's offer.'

'Did you have any involvement with the shop?'

'No, not really,' she said. 'Our family were long-established auctioneers – house clearances and bankrupt stock mainly – Eric and I took the reins when our mother died, but he wanted to sell the more sought-after pieces for higher margins than the hammer price. Consequently, we bought the shop, despite my misgivings, and siphoned off the first rate porcelain and furniture. It never made much money. It might've done well in Manchester or Liverpool, but people round here don't splash out on overpriced antiques, not back then anyway. In the summer of 1970, at the suggestion of our accountant, he converted it into a toy shop and business boomed – right up to the point he boarded it up four years later.'

Colin frowned. 'Why?'

'A question I can't answer with any conviction.'

'He didn't tell you?'

She shook her head. 'He didn't have to; he bought the property outright from the company before converted it. To be honest, I insisted on it. Toys were definitely not us. That said, I gave his new venture my blessing and was pleased to see it do well. As you can imagine, his bizarre business decision came as quite a shock. He refused to discuss the matter, and our relationship went into a swift and terminal decline. His marriage fell apart soon after – she got the house – he moved into the shop and sold all his shares to me, and that was the last contact I had with him. I heard through the grapevine he'd abandoned the shop and moved away, but that was evidently incorrect.'

Colin tried a sympathetic smile before raising his next points. 'The doors and ground floor windows were boarded up from the inside too.'

'Were they?'

'And there are some features upstairs that have *really* intrigued me.'

'What sort of features?'

'Three rooms furnished in very specific period styles.'

She leaned back and sighed. 'Oh dear.'

'Sorry?' Colin said.

She closed her eyes.

'Joyce? Are you okay?'

She nodded slowly. 'Tell me about the rooms.'

'Well … I'm no expert, but one is definitely Edwardian or a little later, one looks Second World War and the third, I'd say, is late 1950s or early 60s.'

She shook her head. 'I suspected it at the time, but I didn't want to believe it.' She stared at the ceiling. 'You needed somewhere to indulge your madcap ideas, didn't you?'

The comment sent a tingle up Colin's spine, but he didn't interrupt.

She glanced at a framed group photograph on a small bureau. 'Shortly after we opened the shop, an old lady died, and her son left the house keys with Eric to price up the contents. He went round there after work and got quite a surprise. Apparently, she must've lived like a modern day Miss Haversham surrounded by furniture and belongings that hadn't changed in nigh on fifty years; he said the entire house seemed frozen in time. The weather was terrible that night, and, by the time he'd finished, it was thundering and lightning and pouring with rain, so he decided to wait it out in the lounge. He got comfortable on the sofa and lit a cigarette; the next thing he knew he was sat at the kitchen table with no idea how he'd got there. On his return home, he started to have flashbacks about the house, but they weren't direct recollections: the furniture was arranged differently and everywhere was lit by natural light. And there were people in there dressed in Edwardian clothing. He said their faces were really clear, but he couldn't recall having had any interaction with them. The next day, the old lady's son came to the office to discuss the valuation, and Eric told him about his experience. At first, the son thought he was having his leg pulled and got quite upset. You see, he'd recognised the descriptions of his parents and him and his sister some forty years before and assumed Eric had seen an old photograph and decided to tease him. We almost lost the sale, and it took some effort to placate him. I knew Eric hadn't meant any harm, but I was angry with him for mentioning it to the customer. He was convinced he'd had a paranormal experience, and I was equally convinced he'd dreamt the whole thing and sleepwalked into the kitchen. We even went round there together, and, low and behold, at the top of the stairs, we found a framed photograph of the very people he'd described.'

'Sounds like autosuggestion.'

'You'd have thought so, wouldn't you? But Eric would have none of it. I appeased him by suggesting the house might've retained an imprint of things that happened long ago, which could play back to a receptive mind in the right conditions.'

'Like falling asleep there during an electrical storm.'

She nodded. 'I even proposed the house had been struck by lightning and given him a bit of a jolt.'

'And how did he feel about that?'

'Let's just say his madcap ideas stem from this particular discussion – at the end of the day, I have a lot to answer for.'

'That seems harsh to me.'

'Maybe, but he did have a fertile imagination, and I put it into overdrive. A week or so after his strange experience, the old lady's house was cleared and put up for sale. That should've been that as far as I was concerned, but Eric had the bit between his teeth. He started to spend a lot of time in libraries, where he claimed to have developed ideas he deemed worthy of investigation. In hindsight, I wish I'd paid more attention when he tried to discuss them with me, but I was trying to run a business with a sibling who was showing less and less interest in it. The *last* thing I wanted was to encourage him.'

'I'd like to know more about his ideas.'

'I'm no expert, far from it, but I can tell you he became convinced that buildings and furnishings weren't just playing back bygone events. To him, they were collectively a sort of doorway to the past.'

'You mean *time travel*?'

'In the bodily sense, no. He believed history could be observed without the observer being seen or sensed;

very much like his first experience, but in a more controlled manner. The furnishings you described must've been an attempt to recreate what happened that night in the old lady's house.'

Colin leaned forward. 'Did the police tell you anything *unusual* about Eric's body?'

'Not that I can recall. Why?'

'There was something on his head.'

'In particular?'

'A wooden frame with battery-powered disks on the inside. The forensic team took it away with them.'

'I can only guess he'd begun to experiment on himself to stimulate the effect.'

'It does seem that way.'

'I wonder if that's what killed him.'

'It was only a small battery, but I wouldn't rule it out.'

'We'll never know for sure.'

'True, but I thought the police would've mentioned it.'

'They probably decided to spare my feelings.'

'How do you mean?'

'Maybe they thought my brother was shielding himself from mind-control rays emitted by flying saucers.'

Colin nodded. 'You might be right.'

'Poor Eric, I hope he's found peace now.'

Colin waited a few moments before he spoke again.

'Joyce, have the police released his body yet?'

'A few days ago – the funeral's on Wednesday.'

'Will you be going?'

She shook her head and turned towards the photograph.

Chapter Nine

Colin pulled onto on the drive, alongside Jan's Ford Focus, and got out of the car.

The quiet cul-de-sac of four-bedroom, detached houses was a pleasant place to come home to at the end of a busy day. But it hadn't been his first choice. Nearly three years ago, when the business really picked up and Jan secured a lucrative promotion, they'd decided to move from their cramped terraced house. Colin had wanted an older property with more land; something with real character, far from the madding crowd. He'd tried so hard to convince Jan, but she'd got her own way in the end.

He waved at a neighbour walking his dog, and locked the car.

Jan put the plate down in front of him and removed the oven glove.

She sat down and poured herself a glass of wine. 'Did you get my text?'

He forked some mashed potato. 'About parents' day?'

'You okay for the third of April?'

'I'll make sure I am.'

'I tried to get hold of you, but your mobile was switched off, and Kath didn't know where you were.'

He gave her an impish wink. 'I was with a woman.'

Jan grinned. 'How long's this being going on?'

'We only met today.'

'Really? Did you catch her name, or was it a cash transaction?'

Brace yourself ...

'Joyce Manning: Eric's octogenarian sister.'

The humour fled from her face.

Here we go ...

'I thought we agreed to move on? Clean slate and all that.'

He shrugged and took a sip of water.

'I hope she told you to mind your own business.'

'Au contraire, mon amore.'

'Let's hear it.'

'She said Eric believed houses and their contents held onto something as they travelled through time, a sort of echo you could tune into to open a window on the past. The weird hat and period piece rooms must've been an attempt to do just that.'

Jan shook her head. 'Sounds like Feng Shui gone mad.'

He smiled. 'I hadn't thought of it like that.'

'But it doesn't mean he was onto something.'

'No smoke without fire.'

'He was a lonely old eccentric who died in his armchair. End of.'

'Old? I doubt he'd reached forty.'

'Some people die of heart attacks in their teens.'

'His body was too far gone to identify the cause of death, and somebody's been using his identity to keep the shop boarded up.'

'I couldn't care less, and neither should you.'

'Bit harsh, Jan.'

'No, Col, it's realistic. The business comes first, not a long-dead eccentric.'

He raised his cutlery in surrender. 'Can't really argue with that, but I need to do a bit more digging. I don't know why, but I feel I owe him that, at least.'

Jan stood up and grabbed her glass. 'Put the dishwasher on when you've finished.'

She strode towards the lounge.

'That programme you wanted to watch starts at eight.'

Part Two

The Auctioneer

Chapter Ten

Wednesday, 26th March

The weather was a funereal cliché: a column of bruised clouds loomed over the skeletal trees at the edge of the graveyard, and a cool wind spat the first flecks of an imminent downpour.

Colin made his way along the line of polished gravestones, towards the huddle of black-clad figures. He stopped ten yards away and pulled up the collar of his jacket.

The priest had a gentle voice.

He that raised up Jesus from the dead will also give life to our mortal bodies, by his Spirit that dwelleth in us.

But the words resonated inside Colin, recalling his father's all too recent passing.

Wherefore my heart is glad, and my spirit rejoiceth; my flesh also shall rest in hope.

He studied the mourners.

Thou shalt show me the path of life; in thy presence is the fullness of joy.

There were only five of them.

And at thy right hand there is pleasure for evermore.

Two middle-aged couples. And an older man; tall and gaunt with a hooked nose.

In sure and certain hope of the resurrection to eternal life.

The priest held out a wooden box.

Through our Lord Jesus Christ, we commend to Almighty God our brother Eric and we commit his body to the ground.

Each, in turn, removed a handful of earth and dropped it into the grave.

Earth to earth, ashes to ashes, dust to dust ...

The older man met Colin's gaze.

The Lord bless him and keep him, the Lord make his face to shine upon him and be gracious unto him.

Colin looked away when the man began to walk towards him.

The Lord lift up his countenance upon him and give him peace. Amen.

Now he felt like an intruder; a morbid voyeur with no business here.

The priest recited the Lord's Prayer to a mumbled, lifeless echo.

Even with a bowed back, the man stood over six feet tall. Swept back, thinning grey hair crowned a wizened face. Hooded, brown eyes fixed Colin with a probing stare. His long woollen coat had seen better days and the knot of his black tie sagged from the frayed collar of an off-white shirt.

'Good morning, Mr Thurcroft,' he said in a gravelly voice. 'I intended to make contact, but you've saved me the trouble.'

Colin grasped the nicotine-yellow fingers with barely disguised reluctance. 'You have the advantage of me.'

The man eased a pack of cigarettes from his coat pocket. 'My name is Ronald Vine – I noticed the recent activity at the shop and made some enquiries.'

'Were you a friend of Eric's?'

He glanced back at the grave. 'I was the only person he trusted.'

'When did you last see him?'

He lit a cigarette with a disposable lighter. 'Nearly forty years ago, but I gather you were acquainted more recently?'

'I wouldn't say *acquainted*. He was practically *mummified*.'

He took a long drag and studied the sky. 'We need to talk.'

'What about?'

'Your personal safety.'

'Why's that any concern of yours?'

'You bought the shop, Mr Thurcroft.'

The brusque tone piqued Colin. 'Come on then, out with it.'

'It mustn't be reopened for any purpose. I would strongly advise you to have it demolished and sell the land to a developer.'

'If this is a joke, your sense of occasion leaves a lot to be desired.'

'This occasion is a joke,' Vine said. 'I almost laughed out loud when the priest commended Eric's soul to God. He'd have to find it first, and I wouldn't wish that on my worst enemy.'

Colin stared open-mouthed at him.

Chapter Eleven

Vine studied his cigarette. 'I thought it best to grab your attention from the start.'

'Mission accomplished,' Colin said. 'You can ditch the melodrama now.'

Vine took a long drag and blew the smoke from his nostrils. 'Selling toys wasn't Eric's only source of income. The Manning family ran a successful auction house, and I was their head auctioneer for over twenty years. I helped him furnish the top floor rooms to very exacting standards. He scrutinised the provenance of every item I requisitioned from the stock list. If there were any doubts or non-original features, however minor, they were rejected outright – '

'Because they retained a temporal link to when they were made?'

Vine narrowed his eyes. 'Now you have the advantage of *me*.'

'I went to see his sister.'

'I see ... how is she?'

'Physically frail, but her mind's still sharp.'

'What exactly did she tell you?'

'Enough to know her brother was convinced he could see the past if he achieved a deep trance in a room filled with furniture from a specific time period. She thought it was ludicrous, and they fell out for good when he shut the shop.'

Vine took another long drag. '*I* was sceptical at first, but his enthusiasm was infectious. He introduced me to philosophical and scientific texts that question the very nature of reality and our interpretation of it; weighty prose, but ultimately rewarding if you stick at it. It genuinely changed my way of thinking, but Eric wasn't satisfied with metaphysical insights; he wanted to tear a hole into the past, which led him inexorably to transcendental meditation and neurology.'

'And what conclusion did he come to?'

'It's not an easy thing to explain.'

'Give it a go.'

'Well … according to Eric, when any three-dimensional object is formed, it makes a sort of imprint that extends into other dimensions we can't see. These dimensions aren't constrained by time in the conventional sense and offer a short cut back to the object's point of creation. With me so far?'

Colin frowned and nodded.

'Eric used furniture, but any object that has survived intact will suffice. Collecting enough of them, from a specific period, in a confined space, amplifies the effect and distorts the way that particular space connects with the unseen dimensions. He called it – let me get this right – a *localised chronospatial fluctuation*. Still with me?'

'Getting the gist of it.'

'His goal was interaction, and he believed it could be accomplished if certain dormant mental acuities were stimulated and controlled.'

'By the battery-powered contraption on his head.'

'Indeed,' Vine said. 'Deep meditation produced some encouraging results, but the helmet was a huge step forward. He was adamant it shouldn't be removed until he'd regained consciousness, whatever the circumstances, and I was under strict instructions to swap the battery if a red light on the circuit board went out.'

'So you were there when he did this?'

Vine nodded. 'It was like a living death; apart from a lowered heart rate, his body seemed to function normally, but Eric was beyond reach. At first, he was confined to the room, but he soon found a way of moving beyond the building and into the streets below, where things looked very different – '

'Weren't you just a *bit* sceptical?'

'Initially, there was doubt on *both* our parts; even Eric wondered if he'd been duped by his own fecund imagination, and we needed a test to prove or disprove it once and for all. The first special room was fitted out with furniture from 1960. At that time, my maternal grandparents lived less than a mile from the shop. I challenged him to go there and tell me what he saw. He returned with a description that was both flawless and highly detailed; he even mentioned their Jack Russell, Nellie, who I took for walks at the weekends.'

'And this convinced you?'

Vine dropped his cigarette and ground it out. 'I'd only suggested it an hour or so before, and there'd never been any reason to even mention my grandparents' home, let alone the furnishings or a dog that died in 1963. It was the day before Christmas Eve, and we got through a full bottle of whiskey that night.'

Colin glanced at the grave. The mourners had gone, and the priest was talking to somebody he assumed to be a grave digger.

'You said Eric's soul couldn't be commended to God.'

Vine nodded and lit another cigarette. 'We came to the conclusion he was experiencing a genuine out of body event. But, one day, he didn't come back. For the best part of two weeks, I spent all my waking hours there, waiting for him to – '

'Whoa, there. Why didn't you get help?'

'He had to return to the fluctuation point to re-join his body. Moving him to a hospital would've sealed his fate and only prolonged the inevitable. I tried to feed him, but he wouldn't even swallow lukewarm soup. I knew it might be dangerous to wake him forcibly, but I was getting desperate. I threw cold water in his face and stuck pins into his skin, but nothing worked. When the end came, I locked up the shop and never went back.'

'You just left him there?'

'I had no choice.'

'What do you mean?'

'This is what I wanted to warn you about. After the visit to my grandparents, Eric was like a man possessed. He took down the hoardings, boarded up the lower floors and moved in a week later. His marriage was in tatters by then, and his wife was glad to see the back of him.' Vine took a long drag. 'We began work on the other special rooms to reach further into the past. Everything went to plan until his third visit to 1920, and the arrival of a bizarre spectacle in the high street. He described it as hundreds of tendrils of fierce blue light arcing around a pitch black hole at its centre. The townsfolk were going about their business seemingly unaware, and, on closer inspection, he realised it was a two dimensional phenomenon bisecting the street. He passed through the hole, into what he described as a dark, lifeless void. He said he'd never felt so utterly alone and in such desperate need of human contact. Then, from nowhere, he sensed another entity close by that absolutely terrified him. He retreated through the light and raced back to the shop. My heart missed a beat when he leapt out of his chair, and he needed a stiff drink before he'd even talk about it. I was convinced he could mentally time travel and was happy to assist him, but this was a bridge too far for me. I said it was a warning; a glimpse of the fate awaiting him if he continued to leave his body.'

'A warning from whom exactly?'

'A higher authority than mortal man, Mr Thurcroft. Unlike me, Eric wasn't a religious man, but he took my advice and made a solemn promise to end his time travelling experiments for good.'

'So why did he renege?'

'Because the entity in the void came back with him.'

Chapter Twelve

Vine glanced at the darkening sky and flicked away his cigarette. 'I think we should get under cover.'

Colin opened his mouth, but the words refused to form.

'The parish hall is open,' Vine said. 'We can find a quiet spot in there.'

They walked along the graves in silence.

Colin mulled over Vine's revelations with growing unease. Although still sceptical, the older man had roused an instinctive fear he hadn't felt since childhood.

When they reached the gravel path, it started to rain and their pace quickened.

The long, red brick building overlooked the small car park at the side of the Gothic church. Inside, no more than a dozen elderly people sat at foldaway tables, chatting over hot drinks and plates of biscuits. Behind a counter at the far end, two rotund women busied themselves with a hissing water boiler and a huge tea pot.

Vine gestured towards a small table near the door. 'Take a seat and I'll get the drinks.' He pulled a battered wallet from his coat. 'Tea or coffee?'

Colin sat down. 'Coffee, please.'

He unbuttoned his coat and watched Vine negotiate the maze of tables and chairs. He glanced at the door, but decided against a swift exit; the revelation heading his way, however irrational, needed to be heard.

Vine returned with two mugs and plastic spoons.

Colin dropped a chipped sugar cube into his grey coffee.

Vine stirred his drink. 'I didn't see Eric for a week or two after that fateful night, but, one day, a colleague told me he'd driven past the shop, and the boards were still in place. This caught me off-guard because Eric had assured me he would reopen as a matter of priority. I phoned him straightaway, but he said he'd been redecorating and restocking and had booked a long holiday in Spain while he still could. I agreed it was a good idea and wished him well. And that was the last conversation we ever had.'

'But you said you were there when he died?'

'I was, but not when he went into that final trance. After two months without a postcard, I tried to phone him, but he didn't pick up. I assumed he hadn't returned, and it was another two weeks before I tried again without success. With the shop boarded up, we'd been using the fire escape to come and go, and I still had a set of keys. I took the next afternoon off and drove into Cranshaw. I called at the local newsagent to buy some cigarettes, and the proprietor asked why I hadn't been in for so long. When I explained that Eric was out of the country, he told me he'd served him regularly during this period and had seen his van reversing into the yard on several occasions. I left without my cigarettes and went straight to the shop, where I found him in the chair in the 1920 room. There was little I could do, so I had a good look around. Nothing unusual came to light until I went into the stockroom and saw that the racking in the far corner had been moved to create space for a large drawing board and a bulky object covered in dustsheets.' Vine reached inside his coat. 'This is what I found underneath.'

Colin took the five dog-eared photographs and studied them one by one.

His first impression was of something not unlike an oversized watch mechanism. A nearby toolbox suggested it was around six feet in diameter and the same in height. A central, gear-driven shaft supported a flat outer ring inset with unfamiliar symbols. The ring passed through four equispaced clusters of radially opposed solenoids mounted on curved brackets extending from the base. The upper half consisted of a bundle of five tubes, wound in dense copper wire, which rose vertically for a couple of feet before splaying outwards like a bouquet of headless flowers. A thick drive belt connected the central shaft to a substantial electric motor mounted on a rusty bracket bolted to the floor.

Vine continued: 'It's not easy to see in the photographs, but the machine had been wired to a junction box and was operated from a hand held device that controlled the speed of the outer wheel and the voltage across the coils. Curiosity got the better of me, so I switched it on and played with the settings. It all seemed to work very smoothly and surprisingly quietly, but its purpose was a complete mystery until I noticed spots of red paint close to each dial. I turned the pointers to line up with them, and, in an instant, the corner of the stockroom collapsed into what I can only describe as a vertical, black ellipse. Sense of depth seemed to flatten out around it like a photograph creased down the middle. There was an odd, ionised taste to the air too. I was absolutely terrified, but then I heard a soft, melodious voice calling my name. It was coming from the ellipse, but I didn't hear it like I'm hearing you now; it seemed to be part of my thoughts, and I felt drawn to it and ready to do its bidding. Thankfully, I came to my senses. I rotated the dials, and everything returned to normal. For what felt like an eternity, I just stared at the wall.'

'Let me get this right.' Colin handed the photographs back. 'Spinning a ring of weird symbols through groups of copper coils caused space to distort and put a voice in your head?'

'In a word, yes.'

Colin took a deep breath. 'This is a lot to take in … '

'The machine had obviously been made in a professional workshop, but the design was not of this world. The five undoubtedly occult symbols confirm that. Eric can only have put it together under the instruction of the entity he'd encountered in the void.'

'Are you saying it *possessed* him?'

'I don't know how they interacted, but there's reason to believe it's still in the shop.'

Colin felt a tingle race up his spine.

'What reason?'

'I'm just coming to that,' Vine said. 'I went back upstairs, but the strange distortions seemed to follow me. They weren't as severe as the one in the stockroom, but I kept catching them at the edge of my vision. It was as if the whole building was pulsing very slowly. The next day, it'd gone, and my attention returned to Eric; however, a couple of days later, it started again. I went down to the stockroom and got the shock of my life: the damn thing was spinning away and the elliptical hole was much larger.'

'And the voice?'

'Truly menacing now. I was told to leave well alone and that my life was in danger if I didn't comply. I switched it off immediately, and everything returned to normal again.'

'Are you absolutely sure Eric hadn't switched it on?'

'Even if he had broken his trance, he was too weak to tackle the stairs.'

'And you've ruled out an accomplice?'

'*I* was the accomplice, Mr Thurcroft; there was nobody else.'

Colin sighed. 'I'm going to wake up in a minute.'

'It's not an easy pill to swallow, but I'm afraid you have no choice.'

'What happened next?'

'I found Eric's Pentax camera and took those photographs as proof of what I'd witnessed. I can't really say why, but I felt it was prudent, especially in light of what I planned to do next.'

'Which was?'

'I stripped it down and took it home. That Sunday, on the pretext of visiting the local tip, I dumped it in a flooded mineshaft at the edge of Cranshaw Heath.'

'The Perch Pond?'

'I didn't know it had a name. You can reach it by car if you use the track that runs down the side of the Black Horse pub.'

'That's the one. I used to fish there when I was a kid. I don't think anybody knows how deep it is, but it's bloody deep.'

'That's what I thought, but there was still more to do. You see, I burned all the drawings and sketches I found in the stockroom, and I searched the top floor thoroughly just to be sure, but I knew the workshop would've made copies. There were a number of invoices from Atkins and Sons on Horsham Road, so I set up a meeting with – '

'Whereabouts on Horsham Road?'

'It's long gone now; there's a care home where it used to be.'

'Derwent Court?'

'That's the one. Why do you ask?'

'Joyce Manning lives there.'

'I didn't know,' Vine said. 'We lost contact when I retired.'

'When did Atkins close down?'

'A good thirty years ago. They never seemed to get back on their feet after Roger Atkins and his eldest son died in the fire at the prototype shop. His wife and brother took over, but it went downhill after that.'

'When did this happen?'

'A few months after I dumped the machine … must've been the October or early November of 1975 because I remember an off-colour joke about them letting their fireworks off too early.' Vine sipped his tea and stared past him. 'I'll never forget driving past and seeing all the girders twisted into strange shapes.'

'That was *some* fire.'

'It was, but the emergency services weren't called. My brother-in-law worked there at the time, and he said it had started at night and burned itself out by morning.'

'And nobody saw the flames and picked up a phone?'

'Apparently not.'

'Doesn't that strike you as odd?'

'I suppose so, but we don't have all the facts.'

Colin frowned. 'You said you set up a meeting.'

'Yes, I saw Roger Atkins under the guise of a patent agent acting on Eric's behalf. He said the original drawings had been returned to him when the work was completed, but they'd made duplicates for the machinists, which he handed over without comment.'

'He didn't ask you anything about the machine?'

'Not that I can remember.'

'Weren't you surprised by that?'

Vine shrugged. 'Not really. In his profession, he must've been aware of the confidentiality surrounding patent applications.'

Colin narrowed his eyes. 'Did he know you were coming for the drawings?'

'Yes, we discussed it over the phone.'

'Giving him ample time to make more copies.'

Vine frowned. 'For what purpose?'

'Think about it,' Colin said. 'The owner and son of the factory that built Eric's machine are killed in the prototype shop by an intense fire nobody noticed.'

Vine nodded slowly. 'In the middle of the night … '

'Exactly.'

'I can see where you're going.'

'I wish *I* did,' Colin said. 'Care to fill me in?'

'Figure of speech, I'm afraid.'

'Let me see those photos again.'

Vine reached inside his coat and passed them to him.

'Can I borrow these?'

'Nothing personal, but I'd rather they stayed with me.'

Colin pulled out his phone. 'Mind if I make copies.'

'For what purpose?'

'To cover my arse.'

Chapter Thirteen

Colin slid the photographs across the table. 'This is the craziest stuff I've ever heard, but, for some reason, I want to give you the benefit of the doubt. That said, you're a long way from convincing me to knock the place down. Even if you did, I wouldn't know where to start with the wife and my bank manager.'

Vine sighed. 'That last night, the night Eric died, the strange pulsing returned, and I sensed something truly malevolent in there. It's hard to describe, but I could almost taste it, and, despite my grief, I was glad to get out. The shop is possessed, Mr Thurcroft; its very structure has been corrupted by the entity.'

Pure conjecture!

'I'd have thought it would've buggered off to find another victim by now.'

'I doubt it's strong enough to roam freely. I can't say how, but the building was altered in some way by the machine and is now its foothold in our world.'

He's on a roll ...

'And it's lurking there still, waiting for its next victim?'

'It bent Eric to its will, and its ultimate purpose is undoubtedly monstrous. There's no reason to believe it won't try again.'

'It couldn't stop you taking the machine or bend you to its will.'

'That's true.' Vine raised his hand to his chest. 'But my faith in the crucifix I've worn all my life would've held it at bay. I'm sure it's what gave me the strength to resist the voice in the stock room.'

Colin decided not to question his religious conviction, but he had the bit between his teeth. 'I've been in there a lot just lately. I lack your faith, and nothing's happened to me.'

'The entity is both cunning and highly intelligent. Be in no doubt, it will pick its victim *and* the moment with due care. In my opinion, the unfortunate individual won't even realise they're being manipulated until it's too late.'

Time to change tack ...

'What do you think the machine was for?'

'To allow the entity to enter our world in a more substantial form, or provide access for something far more terrible.'

Colin shrugged. 'Any ideas?'

Vine fixed him with a hard stare. 'Satan himself, Mr Thurcroft.'

Goodnight and God bless ...

Colin drained his lukewarm coffee. 'So you hotfooted it out of there and left him to rot in that chair.'

'It's haunted me ever since. But what else could I do? Going to the authorities would've implicated me in Eric's death, but that wasn't my main concern. What I dreaded the most was having the situation taken out of my control and my protests dismissed as the ranting of a mad man. I did consider exorcism, but what would I tell the priest? And how do you explain the corpse in the chair?'

'Surely you could've disposed of the body.'

Vine winced and shook his head. 'The more I thought about it, the more I realised that leaving well alone was the best option in the circumstances.'

'So the shop became his mausoleum.'

Vine frowned. 'I suppose so ... '

'Sat there with that bloody helmet on his head.'

'I had planned to take it with me, but I was somewhat preoccupied that last night. A few weeks went by before it even crossed my mind, and, by then, I'd missed my chance – he would've been too far gone, and I didn't want to remember him that way – to be absolutely honest, I didn't have the stomach for it, with or without the malevolent entity.'

Colin folded his arms on the table. 'Then you stole Eric's identity and emptied his bank account to stop the compulsory purchase.'

Vine nodded. 'I'm not proud of that, but I had to keep people away. I *can* say, hand on heart, that I made no personal profit from it. All his savings, and some of my own, went to fight the council and repair the worst of the vandalism.'

'Why didn't you just burn it down and have done with it?'

'I did consider it, but anything less than the complete destruction of the property wouldn't have sufficed. I'd no idea how to ensure a sturdy, three-storey building would, quite literally, burn to the ground despite the best efforts of the fire brigade.'

'But you couldn't maintain the status quo indefinitely.'

'Maybe not,' Vine said. 'But the council seemed to have lost interest, and I was hoping it would deteriorate to the point where they'd have to demolish it regardless.'

'What if the property survives you? No offence, but there's a good chance it will.'

'My solicitor is under instruction to issue a sealed caveat emptor to anybody that purchased it after my

64

death. It was far from the perfect solution, but I really didn't know what else to do.'

'I understand you hadn't corresponded with Eric's solicitors for quite some time.'

Vine nodded. 'I kept contact to a practical minimum.'

'Did you know they'd thrown the towel in?'

'They sent numerous letters to the PO Box I set up for correspondence, but I seldom check these days, and it was several months before I read them – the coffers were bare and wheels were in motion. My only option was to keep an eye on the shop.'

'I really upset the apple cart, didn't I?'

'Didn't you just?'

Colin sighed. 'What the hell have I got myself into?'

'A dangerous mess that my recommendation would resolve.'

'Easier said than done, my friend. Look, I need time to get my head around this. How about we meet up again in a week or so?'

'Can we agree that you'll keep away from the shop until then?'

'My distribution manager is in there now, sorting through the old stock. Next week, I've got site meetings with the architect and several builders.'

'Is your manager alone?'

'Strictly speaking, he should have one of the warehouse lads with him.'

'Give him a call.'

'And say what?'

Vine shrugged. 'Ask for a progress report. If he's experienced anything unusual, I'm sure he'll let you know.'

Colin tapped his phone and held it to his ear. He played with his mug for a few moments, and then rolled his eyes. 'It's gone to voicemail.'

Vine stood up. 'I suggest we get round there.'

'Cool your boots. He's got form for leaving his phone around.'

'Nevertheless.'

'I'll try him again in ten minutes.'

'After everything I've told you, do you want to take the risk?'

Colin sighed and got to his feet. 'Where're you parked?'

Vine turned to go. 'I walked here.'

He fastened his coat and followed him.

Chapter Fourteen

Colin slowed the car when they turned onto Endell Street. The yard gates were wide open, and one of the company vans had been reversed inside.

He turned to Vine. 'Well, he's still here.'

Vine met his gaze but remained silent.

He drove around to the front and parked.

Vine got out and walked towards the shiny steel security door.

He wrapped it with his knuckles. 'Did the council fit this?'

Colin flicked the key fob. 'Had no choice; they trashed the original.' He reached into his pocket for the keys. 'Looks different with the boards off, doesn't it?'

Vine stepped back and surveyed the shop. 'Indeed it does.'

Inside, Colin was struck by the deathly silence.

He led Vine through the wooden counter and a set of double doors.

The stockroom was crisscrossed by deep shadows, but Colin could see that twenty or so cardboard boxes had been taken down from the racking and their contents stacked on the floor. His heart missed a beat when he noticed, for the first time, the folded drawing board propped against the far wall.

'Alan!' he shouted. 'I know you're in here!'

Silence.

'Try his mobile again,' Vine said.

Colin tapped his phone. A few moments later, Alan Sharrock's discordant ringtone assaulted their ears, and a blue glow lit the top of a small box.

He strode towards it and retrieved the phone. 'Eight missed calls. Fuck's sake!'

When it became clear there was nobody on the second floor, the lightness in Colin's stomach turned to queasiness. Vine made no comment and led the way to the top floor.

In the corridor, he turned to Colin. 'Is the 1920 room still in the state you found it?'

'The only thing missing is Eric. Why?'

Vine's complexion lost what little colour it had. 'I'll check the other rooms.'

Colin gave the kitchen a quick once-over, and then went into the next room.

Nothing looked out of place until he glanced at the chair Eric Manning had died in. He'd covered it with a tarpaulin sheet to hide the stains, but it was obvious someone had sat there since; and a helmet, identical to the one he'd seen on the corpse, rested on the arm.

Chapter Fifteen

Colin picked up the helmet and went to the window.

A few moments later, Vine made a wary entry and stared at the armchair.

Colin glared at him. 'Something you want to tell me?'

'About what?'

He held out the helmet. 'The police took the one he was wearing.'

Vine turned towards him. 'Where did you find that?'

'On the arm of the chair.'

Vine approached and took it from him. 'It must be the other one.'

'He had a *spare*?'

'It was meant for me. Eric wanted me to travel with him, but I – '

'Well it wasn't here yesterday.' Colin pointed at the chair. 'And somebody's been sat in that chair.'

'You don't think I had anything to do with it?'

'You've got keys.'

Vine looked crestfallen. 'I resent the accusation, Mr Thurcroft. Even if I *had* a motive, the fire escape is a death trap.'

Colin chewed his lip. 'Does anybody else know what you've told me?'

Vine shook his head. 'Definitely not. I really have no – '

The rumble of footsteps on the stairs cut him short.

'Stay here,' Colin said. 'Let me handle this.'

He reached the corridor as Alan Sharrock opened the stairwell door.

'Alright, Col? Wasn't expecting you.'

'There's some stuff to do before I meet the builders.'
Colin pulled Alan's phone from his pocket and lobbed
it to him. 'I *did* ring you.'

Alan snatched it from the air. 'Sorry, mate. I've been
at the walk in centre.'

'Are you okay?'

'I'm fine, but young Josh is in a bit of a two and
eight.'

'How do you mean?'

'I found him slumped against the wall, more or less
where you're standing.'

Colin felt his blood turn to ice.

'What happened?'

'I think he just fainted, but he's very confused.'

'What was he doing up here?'

'He was only getting in the way, so I let him have a
mooch round.'

Colin ran his fingers through his hair. 'Jesus H … '

'He's waiting to see somebody now, so I'll have to
get off. I only popped back for my mobile, but then I
saw your car out front.'

'Have you let his parents know?'

'No, he didn't want me too.'

'Okay, mate, I'll finish up and get over there.'

Alan turned to go. 'Cheers, Col.'

When his footfalls subsided, Colin returned to the
room.

Vine was sitting on the chaise longue with the
helmet on his lap.

'Did you hear any of that?' Colin said.

He nodded. 'Every word.'

Colin went to the window. 'This is bad, really
fucking bad.'

'We don't know what happened yet. There may be–'

He spun around. 'Turn it on.'

'Sorry?'

'*Turn* the helmet on.'

Vine flicked a switch at the back, and a small red light glowed on the circuit board.

'That's a surprise,' he said. 'The battery should be flat by now.'

'Of course it should,' Colin said. 'But somebody fitted a new one.'

Vine squinted at the back. 'Are you sure?'

'What do you think a battery would look like after forty years?'

Vine sighed. 'You're right ... it's a brand new Duracell.'

Colin scowled. 'And there's *nothing* you can tell me?'

'I'm lost for words.'

'This'll have to wait,' he said. 'I need to get down to the walk in centre.'

Vine got to his feet. 'Give me your phone number first.'

Colin waited for the sluggish glass doors to part, and then headed towards the reception window. A dour young woman pointed him to a large room, where rows of seated people faced a wide desk occupied by several receptionists. It was about half full, and only the occasional cough punctuated the air of stoic malaise.

Alan Sharrock waved from the back row.

Colin eased passed an elderly couple and sat down next to him. 'What's the score?'

'He's with a nurse now. I offered to go in with him, but he said he'd be okay.'

'What *exactly* happened?'

'I only brought him with me because the insurance won't let me pull boxes off a shelf on my own. I could see he was getting bored, so I let him have a wander while I got on with it. Ten minutes later, he nipped out for a can of coke and a coffee for me, and then I didn't hear from him for a good half hour. Cut a long story short, I found him on the floor outside the kitchen. He was conscious but very groggy, so I took him outside for some fresh air. He recovered quickly enough, but when he said he couldn't remember anything since we arrived, I brought him here to get checked out.'

'Any idea what he was up to?'

'Haven't a clue and neither has he.'

Colin chewed his lip.

'There is one thing though,' Alan said. 'When we checked in at the front desk, he gave the wrong name. He corrected himself straightaway, but it was odd; I mean it didn't sound anything like Josh.'

'What name did he give?'

'Eric.'

Chapter Sixteen

Colin felt his blood freeze again.

'Are you sure he said *Eric*?'

'Yeah, I'm sure, and I've already made the connection.'

'What connection?'

'The guy who died up there was called Eric, wasn't he?'

'Where're we going with this?'

'You tell me, Col.'

Colin sighed. 'How much does Josh know?'

'He'd heard rumours about the body, and I put him straight on one or two details that were way off the mark.'

'Does he know Eric's name?'

Alan shrugged. 'I might've mentioned it.'

'There you go then. If he's been prowling around up there with an overactive imagination, who knows what effect it's had.'

Alan frowned. 'I'm assuming he's not *on* anything. If you know what I mean?'

'He doesn't come across like that, but you never know these days.'

'Have you noticed anything unusual?'

'With Josh?'

Alan's eyes met his. 'No, in the *shop*.'

'Don't be daft.'

'You've been reluctant to clear that furniture.'

'We've done that to death, mate.'

'If you say so.'

'I don't believe in ghosts, Alan, and neither do you.'

They didn't speak for a couple of minutes; enough time for Colin's thoughts to wind into a knot of disquieting conjecture.

He jumped when Alan nudged him.

Josh Lathom was talking to a male nurse outside one of the examination rooms.

Colin and Alan made their way to the door, where Josh met them with a sheepish expression. He was a little paler than usual, and his tousled hair cried out for gel.

'How're you feeling?' Colin said.

'Blood pressure's a bit low, but I'm okay.'

'What did the nurse say?'

'Don't skip breakfast and see the doctor if it happens again.'

'Have you fainted before?'

Josh shook his head. 'Never.'

'Alan said you gave the wrong name when you checked in.'

'Yeah … don't know what happened there. Well weird.'

Colin patted his arm. 'Come on, I'll run you home.'

Colin watched Josh to his parents' front door, and then parked around the corner. He found Vine's number on his phone and drummed the steering wheel as it rang.

'Hello?'

'It's Colin Thurcroft.'

'How is he?'

'He told the receptionist his name was Eric.'

Silence.

'Mr Vine?'

'I'm still here.'

'I've just dropped him home. He's been given the all clear, but he still can't remember what happened.'

'There can be little doubt he used the helmet.'

'Alan said he nipped out to buy drinks, but it must've been a ruse to get a battery.'

'Without question,' Vine said. 'Was he wearing it when he was found?'

'Alan would've mentioned it.'

'Then he must've removed it when he came to and placed it on the chair.'

'And then fainted in the corridor.'

'It would seem so.'

'Where did Eric keep that helmet?'

'Somewhere safe, but I really can't remember.'

'Yet Josh managed to find it.'

'He had a helping hand, Mr Thurcroft. This is what I was trying to warn you about.'

'If only you'd done it sooner.'

'Regrettably, I have to agree … '

'But why him?' Colin said. 'Why not Alan? And what about me? I've been in there a dozen times.'

'How old is Josh?'

'Just turned eighteen.'

'Maybe his young mind was more susceptible.'

Colin shut his eyes and blew out his cheeks. His twelve-year-old daughter, and only child, had been pestering him to take her to the shop to look at the old toys.

Vine continued: 'We can nip this in the bud by ensuring he never sets foot in there again, but his use of Eric's name is troubling.'

'I can't quite believe I'm asking you this, but do you think they met during the trance?'

'Yes, I do, which means Eric's soul is still in limbo.'

Colin sighed. 'What *have* I got myself into?'

'Keep an eye on him and inform me of any developments. And please don't say a word to anybody about this, not even your wife.'

'She wouldn't believe me if I did.'

'I assume this has convinced you to shut the place up, at least until you've had time to think things through.'

'You assume right.'

'What're you going to do with the helmet?'

Colin visualised the plastic bag in the boot. 'I'll keep it safe for now.'

'Let me know what you decide about the shop.'

'We'll talk again soon.'

'Take care, Mr Thurcroft.'

'Bye, Mr Vine.'

Colin tapped the screen and closed his eyes.

Chapter Seventeen

Holly Thurcroft, dressed in her favourite pink onesie, sauntered into the study. 'What're you up to, Dad?'

Colin minimised the image on the laptop. 'None of your beeswax, Nosey.'

She leaned on his shoulder and grabbed the A4 sheet. 'Is it Chinese writing?'

'No, Love, I was thinking about changing the logo.'

'Why?'

Oh what a tangled web we weave!

'Well – we've got the shop now, and stuff that works on a website doesn't always look good on a building.'

That almost convinced me.

'Five weird shapes won't work.'

'I was only going to use *one* of them.'

'Did you copy them?'

'No. Why do you ask?'

She dropped the sheet onto the desk. 'Think I've seen them before.'

His fingers tightened around the pen. 'Have you?'

'Maybe not *exactly* the same, but *quite* like them.'

'Where was this?'

'One of the documentary channels. Discovery, I think ... or History.'

'What was it about?'

'It was ages ago, Dad. I can't remember.'

'Try.'

'Why's it so important?'

'Because I'll end up in court for copyright infringement, that's why.'

'What's that?'

'Doesn't matter, but it's something I'd rather avoid.'

'Kirsty was with me.' Her eyes brightened. 'I'll text her.'

She left the room, and he turned his attention to the symbols.

Her revelation had intrigued him, but he wasn't expecting an insight into the workings of Eric Manning's bizarre machine. Holly's vivid imagination was something her parents had learned to handle with a generous pinch of salt. That said, it was the only lead he had.

A couple of minutes later, she returned wearing one of her exaggerated frowns.

'She says she can't remember.'

He sighed. 'Talk to her tomorrow. See if you can jog her memory.'

'Okay – I'll try.'

'Isn't it about time you were turning in?'

She pecked him on the cheek. 'Night, Dad.'

'Goodnight, Love – sleep tight.'

Chapter Eighteen

Thursday, 27th March, 8.56am

Ronald Vine stepped into his slippers and went to the front door. He attached the security chain and opened it a few inches.

The pale youth, in the tight jeans and woollen top, didn't look like he was about to launch into a sales pitch or guilt trip him into a direct debit.

'What do you want?' Vine said.

The youth flashed a brief smile 'Hello, Ron.'

Vine's chest tightened. 'Do I know you?'

'I'm the Ghost of Christmas Past.'

He dropped the security chain. 'You'd better come in.'

Colin waited for the fork lift truck to trundle past, and then strode into the warehouse.

Alan Sharrock was leaning over a large cardboard box with his phone at his ear.

He straightened up as Colin approached and rolled his eyes. 'I know, I know, but we need it sorted today – yeah – yeah – okay, bye.' He ended the call and shook his head.

'Problem?'

'Two hundred Berghaus RG1s, all small.'

'And we ordered?'

'Hundred each in medium and large.'

'Who signed for them?'

'Good question.'

'What do you mean?'

'Should've been Josh, but nobody's seen him all morning.'

'Have you tried his mobile?'

Alan nodded. 'A few times.'

Colin reached into his jacket. 'I'll try his parents.'

'He mightn't be fully recovered from yesterday.'

'So why no phone call?'

Alan shrugged. 'It is a bit out of character.'

Colin's phone rang before he found the number. The screen displayed "Vine".

'Hello?'

'It's Ronald Vine, Mr Thurcroft. I have a visitor.'

'Sorry?'

'A young man of your acquaintance.'

'When did he arrive?'

'A few minutes ago, but he wants to speak to both of us.'

'What's your address?'

'Twenty-four, Carmarthen Street.'

'I'm on my way.'

He ended the call and turned to go. 'Something's come up, Alan. I'll catch you later.'

'What about Josh?' Alan called.

'Leave it with me,' he replied without looking back. 'I've got it covered.'

Colin got out of the car and surveyed the tree-lined street of pre-war detached houses. Ronald Vine's property stood out like a rotten tooth in a Hollywood smile. Scaly windows nestled into sooty brickwork under a sagging roof, and a bloated hedge threatened to burst through the crooked front wall.

The squealing, rusty gate opened onto a path of cracked, weed-choked flags. He followed its gentle sweep to a weathered black door and rapped the knocker.

Vine opened the door and beckoned him into a gloomy hallway.

'How is he?' Colin said.

'Physically, he seems fine, but his mind is hidden to us.'

'Hidden?'

'He did indeed meet Eric during the trance, but that wasn't the end of it.'

'Get to the point.'

'Two souls occupy his body. Currently, the one I knew as Eric Manning holds sway.'

Chapter Nineteen

Colin followed Vine into a spacious lounge ringed by tall bookcases and dark bureaus. A sturdy Chesterfield suite enclosed an old radiant fire in a mantel of boldly carved wood. Framed prints of pastoral oil paintings dotted the sombre wallpaper. Winding veins of cigarette smoke transfused the cool air.

Josh was sitting in an armchair with its back to the bay window.

Vine sat down on the sofa. 'Eric, this is Colin Thurcroft.'

Colin perched on the other armchair and studied Josh. He didn't look any different, but his posture and expression were those of a more mature and self-confident man.

'Good morning, Colin,' Josh said. 'It's good to meet you in the flesh, so to speak.'

The voice was Josh's, but the phrasing wasn't.

Colin opened his mouth, but the words refused to form.

Vine seemed to sense his discomfort. 'Before you arrived, I was told things that only Eric could know; things we said and witnessed over forty years ago. I know it's hard to believe, but I'm absolutely convinced he's speaking through this young man.'

Colin took a deep breath. 'This is madness ... '

Josh leaned forward. 'Let me start by saying Josh Lathom hasn't been harmed by my presence, nor will he remember any of today's events. When I've said what needs to be said, I'll leave his body never to return.'

'Right then,' Colin said. 'Let's hear it.'

'Ron tells me that you're up to speed with the events surrounding my physical death.'

He nodded.

'Then it's time to come clean, gentlemen.' He cleared his throat. 'The machine wasn't built under coercion or supernatural possession; I did it gladly because I believed it was the right thing to do.'

Vine narrowed his eyes. 'But what about the entity in the void?'

'There was no void, Ron. And no evil demon to scare me away.'

'Then why did you say there was?'

'Because I was told to.'

'By who?'

Josh flashed a wry smile. 'Who indeed.'

An uneasy silence ensued.

'Sorry, Ron,' he said. 'Believe me, it was nothing personal.'

Vine shrugged his shoulders. 'So what *did* happen that night?'

'Well, there *was* that strange light show across the high street. That much is true. But when I went through the eye of it, I found myself in a circular room bathed in an ethereal, bluish glow. It was featureless except for five grey symbols around the periphery. One of them changed into a rectangular doorway, and a man entered and approached me. He was about six feet tall and slimly built, but that's about as much as I could say for sure. He was wreathed in the same bluish glow, which blurred his features to such an extent I wasn't even sure if he was clothed or naked. He began to communicate with me, but it wasn't English by any means; more of a psychic stream of images and emotions that I immediately understood. He said he was one of five

83

beings who were trapped between dimensions after a failed teleportation experiment – '

'To and from where exactly?' Colin said.

'He didn't say, but they wanted my help to return home, wherever that might be.'

'And you agreed?'

'It was hard to say no to what I judged to be a pacific and intelligent entity in a desperate situation. He said that our material world ran parallel to theirs, and the machine they wanted me to build would allow them to effectively jump across. He bought my secrecy with a promise of technical know-how that would make me rich beyond the dreams of avarice. He even suggested the story I told Ron. Consequently, when I got back to the shop, I broke the trance and deliberately leapt out of the chair to convince him I was really scared.'

'It worked,' Vine said.

'I know, 'Josh said and smiled. 'But I genuinely needed that whisky.'

Colin frowned. 'I get the impression this meeting wasn't a coincidence.'

Josh nodded. 'Apparently, they sensed my presence some weeks before and set about creating an interface to make contact.'

'And the machine?'

'With Ron out of the way, I made frequent visits to receive instructions from the blue man and his companions. The mental images they implanted were crystal clear and allowed me to create detailed drawings for Atkins and Sons to work to. Roger Atkins was a bit wary when he saw how strange the components were, but cash up front and a bit of flannel got the job done. I put it together in the stockroom and made sure everything worked okay. Under their guidance, I tweaked the configurations until a partial warp was achieved. And then everything changed … '

Colin and Vine exchanged glances.

Josh continued: 'They prevented me from returning to my body, and, by the time Ron arrived to wreck their plans, it was too late. The machine had created a permanent but rather weak doorway, but it was guarded by them, and I had no living body to return to. I didn't know *what* to do, to be honest, so I watched and waited from a distance. Shortly after, I sensed something close by: a disturbance with all the characteristics of another much bigger doorway. The blue light moved towards it, and I followed, but they went through and shut the door behind them. Then it was just a case of hanging around for a suitable mind to interact with.'

'You *hung around* for forty years?'

'Time flows oddly when you're out of body. It was a huge shock to realise that four decades had passed in what felt like a few months to me.'

Colin frowned. 'I take it Josh was more susceptible than us?'

'Yes, he was. It might be down to his youth, but it was relatively straightforward to influence his actions through the doorway. Once he'd got the helmet to work, I slipped into his mind without him even knowing.'

'So the entities are gone for good?'

'Gone from the limbo land I was trapped in, but their ultimate destination and purpose are anybody's guess. They may've only wanted to return home, but their callous behaviour when the machine was ready suggests otherwise. I strongly suspect the doorway they escaped through led to our world and was created by someone at their bidding.'

'Any ideas?'

'I'm afraid not, but you need to – '

Josh cried out and arched his back.

Colin leapt to his feet.

Josh fell back into the chair and raised a hand.

'He's starting to fight me,' he gasped. 'I can't stay much longer.'

Chapter Twenty

Colin sat down and looked at Vine. The older man's eyes didn't leave Josh.

Josh took a couple of deep breaths. 'I needed to make you aware of this.'

Colin shrugged. 'And how do you propose we act on it?'

'If I tell you everything I know, you might be able to find signs of their presence and warn the authorities.'

'Forty years on, don't you think we'd know about it by now?'

'Not necessarily. They may have long term plans that are anything but obvious.'

Colin blew out his cheeks.

'What else can you tell us?' Vine said.

'The machine synchronises the rotation of five pure iron, geometric forms through four oscillating magnetic fields. This deceptively simple premise, when executed in a precisely controlled manner, can create localised spatial distortions that open into dimensions we don't normally perceive.'

'These forms,' Colin said. 'They're the strange symbols on the outer wheel, yeah?'

Josh nodded.

'And the ones you saw in the circular room?'

'The same.'

Colin shifted in his chair. 'Is there a connection between their technology and your use of objects from the same time period?'

'Without doubt,' Josh said. 'The juxtaposition of chronologically contiguous forms with a brain stimulated by a controlled electromagnetic waveform has to be rooted in the same core principle, whatever that might be.'

'I think I got *most* of that.'

'Let's just say the fact they made contact during one of my trans-dimensional trips is highly significant.' Josh winced and gripped the arms of the chair. 'My time is getting near. If you need to ask me anything, I suggest you – '

'Something's just occurred to me,' Colin said. 'The other doorway might've been closer than you think.'

'Sorry?'

'I'm more or less convinced Roger Atkins built a copy of the machine that destroyed the prototype shop along with him and his son.'

'When did this happen?'

'A few months after you died.'

Josh narrowed his eyes and turned to Vine.

Vine nodded. 'The heat warped the steel girders, but nobody reported the alleged fire until they saw the devastation in the morning.'

Josh shook his head. 'Why would he do something like that?'

'Who knows?' Colin said. 'Maybe they were just curious.'

'This could be your starting point.'

'Assuming the entities survived the destruction.'

'True,' Josh said. 'But don't rule out a deliberate ploy to cover their tracks.'

Nobody spoke for a few moments.

Josh winced again. 'It's time to go, gentlemen.'

'Where to?' Vine said.

'I don't know, Ron. Another form of existence or utter oblivion awaits – I touched on something out there I can't describe; something infinite yet oddly familiar, maybe even sentient. I can imagine what you're thinking, but *God* isn't the word I'm dancing around. There're simply no words to describe it.'

'Words *would* fail you in the presence of the Almighty.'

'I wish I had your faith, Ron.'

'I'll pray for you anyway,' Vine said. 'I believe we'll meet again.'

Josh smiled and shut his eyes. 'You never know … '

A few moments later, he rolled forward onto the floor.

Chapter Twenty-one

Colin lifted Josh onto the chair and held his wrist. 'Skin's like ice, but I can feel a pulse.'

Vine went to the window and lit a cigarette. 'How do we explain how he got here?'

'I'll think of something.'

'We should get him into your car.'

'And what if somebody sees us?'

'It'll give the curtain twitchers something to gossip about.'

'Who to? The police?'

Josh grunted.

Colin patted his cheek. 'Josh?'

His eyes flickered open and darted around the room. 'Where am I?'

'Carmarthen Street.'

Josh stared at him. 'What?'

'It's okay, mate – you're absolutely fine – a Good Samaritan found you stumbling around in the road. You said you were lost and had to get to work, so he brought you to his home and phoned me.'

'How long have I been out?'

'Not long – looks like you had a repeat of yesterday.'

With a little help from Colin, Josh got to his feet.

He took a deep breath and swivelled his neck. 'I need a piss.'

'Up the stairs,' Vine said distractedly. 'Second on the left.'

Colin guided him to the door. 'Take your time – splash some water on your face.' He watched him to the landing, and then joined Vine at the window. 'Thank God he's okay.'

'He'll be fine; you're bullet proof at that age.'

They didn't speak for a few moments.

Vine turned to Colin. 'At least you can get on with the shop now.'

'That's true.'

'I trust it will keep you busy for some time, but we need to think long and hard about what Eric said and how to act on it.'

Colin nodded. 'It does need some discussion.'

'In the meantime, I'm going to pay Joyce Manning a visit.'

'What for?'

'Don't worry, I don't intend to divulge what happened here, but we need her consent to release the other helmet from the police. After today, we've a duty to ensure it doesn't fall into the wrong hands.'

'You've lost me.'

'The police report will describe exactly how Eric was found. It is effectively a set of instructions on how to do what he did, and who knows what else might be lurking at the edge of our perception.'

'Bit of a longshot, if you ask me.'

'Perhaps, but I don't think we should take the risk.'

'And you can't ask her outright. As far as she's concerned, only the police and the people who found him know anything about it.'

'Ways and means, Mr Thurcroft.' Vine tapped his nose. 'I always got on well with Joyce. I'll start with a trip down memory lane and take it from there.'

'Assuming you get permission, do you really want to announce yourself to police officers investigating Eric's stolen identity?'

'They've nothing on me.'

'That might change if you ask for that particular item.'

Vine frowned and turned towards the window. 'Let me think about it.'

Colin went to the door. 'I'd better check on him.' He reached for the handle, and then stopped and turned around. 'Just one more thing: do you mind if we progress to first name terms? I think we can dispense with formalities now.'

'Of course – Ron or Ronald is fine with me.'

He smiled and left the room.

Colin stepped out of the front door and turned towards Sally Lathom. 'Like I said, I don't want to see him before Monday whatever the doctor says.'

'I'm hoping he'll be okay by then.'

He nodded. 'So am I, but it won't hurt him to have a break.'

She smiled warmly. 'Thanks for bringing him back.'

'No problem at all.'

'I'll be in touch.'

He turned to go. 'Bye, Sally.'

'Thanks again.'

He raised his hand and plucked the car keys from his pocket.

Colin found Alan Sharrock in the warehouse and told him the same story he'd told Josh and his mother. When he got into the office, Kath informed him of several calls which needed his immediate attention and pointed him to a teetering stack of mail on his desk.

It was just after one when he checked his texts.

He read the one from Holly first: *kirsty remembered tell u 2nite xx H*

He called her mobile.

'Dad, I'm going into Maths.'

'Okay, Love, but can you just tell me what she said.'

'It was a programme about supernatural mysteries.'

'And where do the symbols come in?'

'Some men saw them on a crashed UFO.'

'Are you *sure*?'

'Yeah, I remembered it when she told me.'

'Which programme was this?'

He heard a door slam, and a deep male voice said something unintelligible.

'Dad, I have to go.'

'Talk tonight, yeah?'

'Bye, Dad.'

'Bye … '

He tapped the screen and placed the phone on the desk.

Kath popped her head around the door. 'Got a minute?'

He met her gaze and nodded.

'You okay?' she said. 'You look like you've seen a ghost.'

'Twice in one day.'

'Sorry?'

He summoned a smile. 'Doesn't matter.'

Chapter Twenty-two

Colin typed "UFO Crash 1951" and hit return. 'Is there *nothing* else you can tell me?'

Holly shrugged and shook her head.

'Are you absolutely sure?'

'I've told you everything.'

'Tell me again.'

She sighed. 'It was nineteen fifty something, there were two men hunting in the woods in America, and they found a UFO on the ground with symbols on it like yours.'

He perused the screen and frowned.

'Dad?' she said, stretching the vowel to breaking point.

'What?'

'Your symbols can't be the *same* as the ones on the UFO.'

'Why do you say that?'

'How could they be? It's too much of a coincidence.'

She's got a point ...

'Better to be safe than sorry.'

She rolled her eyes. 'Can I go now?'

He nodded without taking his eyes from the screen.

She swept out of the room. 'Laters.'

'Laters, Hol ... '

He reached the fifth page and decided to move on to 1952, but, as he grabbed the mouse, one of the results caught his eye.

Crash in the Cascades 1951...

He clicked on the link to a no frills web page and read the report with dispassionate curiosity, but his heart began to thump when he cross checked the embedded image of the five symbols with his own sketches.

He leaned back and ran his fingers through his hair.

His well-honed scepticism had never taken such a battering. With some effort, he marshalled his mangled thoughts, but they were devoid of a rational explanation to counter the stark revelation writ large on the screen of his laptop.

What have I got myself into?

He got up and shut the study door, and then found Vine's number on his phone.

He chewed his lip as it rang and rang.

'Hello?'

'Ron, it's Colin. Sorry it's a bit late, but I've found a connection with the symbols on the machine.'

'You work quickly.'

'I forgot to tell you, my daughter saw me sketching them last night and said she'd seen them before on a TV documentary. She wasn't even sure which channel it was, but I learned enough to do some internet research. It turns out they're just about exact matches for ones seen on a downed UFO in Oregon in 1951.'

Silence.

'Ron?'

'Sorry – I just needed a moment to digest that.'

'Are you okay to run through it now?'

'Yes, I'd like to hear it.'

'According to this website, it's an obscure and discredited incident that has been sidestepped by the more reputable UFO researchers.'

'Not a good start,' Vine said. 'But I'm listening.'

Colin scanned the screen. 'It begins with two men on a hunting trip in the Cascades. Three days in, they were woken early by military helicopters flying just above the trees. The aerial activity spooked the game, but it'd died away by midday when they stopped to eat on a high ridge and noticed something glinting in the valley below. At first, they thought it might be a stream or a small lake, but the map showed neither at that location. They decided to check it out and climbed down into the valley, where they quickly lost their bearings. At the point of turning back, they came across a long straight line of broken conifers. They followed it to a clearing that'd been ripped in two by a wide gouge. At its furthest extent, a large metallic sphere lay partially buried in the ground. When they got closer, they realised it wasn't a smooth sphere; more like what they called a huge soccer ball, about twenty feet in diameter, made up of five and six sided plates. It was emitting a faint, pulsating hum, but they saw no signs of damage or any discernible features; no windows or doors, or any recognisable propulsion system. One of the men, Seth Hartford, took photographs with a camera he'd brought along to record their kills. Apparently, he only noticed a strange symbol on each of the hexagonal plates when he viewed them at a certain angle. He counted five distinct types in total. After around ten minutes, soldiers appeared at the edge of the clearing, and they fled the scene. The woods were crawling with troops, but Hartford managed to hide the camera in a tree before they were surrounded. An unnamed major arrived and told them they'd witnessed the aborted test flight of a top secret aircraft and were not to breathe a word to anyone on pain of death. Then they were marched to an old fire road and bundled into a Jeep with two soldiers, who drove them to a place called Culp Creek, where Hartford had left his pick-up truck. The Jeep tailed them all the way to Eugene, some forty miles way. Hartford returned a few months later to retrieve the camera. He went back to the clearing and found the gouge filled in and replanted with grass and bushes; even the damaged trees had been replaced.'

'Is this Hartford's personal account?' Vine said.

'It is, but he kept quiet for twenty years.'

'What about his companion?'

'He isn't named and apparently died of liver failure in the early sixties. Hartford claimed it was due to heavy drinking that started soon after. In 1971, Hartford suffered a severe stroke and decided to go public while he still could. He made contact with a UFO investigator, named Bill Klein, and told him everything. During their one and only meeting, Hartford showed Klein the photographs, which he claimed were developed in his own dark room. Klein wasn't allowed to take them away but made several sketches that he published in a book called *Down to Earth* in 1973 – he was desperate to include the photographs, but Hartford wanted an enormous sum that Klein had no way of raising – '

'How much?' Vine said.

'Half a million dollars. Silly money now, but it must've been an astronomical figure back then. Armed with only Hartford's vague directions, Klein spent the best part of a year in a fruitless search for the crash site and somebody to corroborate the story. He wrote several letters to Hartford, imploring him to reconsider, but he wouldn't budge. Hartford died just before the book was published without disclosing the whereabouts of the photographs.'

'It's easy to see why this story isn't taken seriously.'

'I agree,' Colin said. 'But that's not the end of it. A few months after the book hit the shelves, Klein received an anonymous phone call from a man who claimed to have worked on the crashed sphere. They eventually met in a remote spot in Nevada, where he was allegedly told a truly remarkable story.'

'Allegedly?'

'Afraid so,' Colin said. 'Klein went missing soon after and hasn't been seen since. Only his daughter knew about the meeting, but he'd kept her in the dark about the details. Apparently, she tried in vain to subpoena various government departments until her death in a somewhat suspicious traffic accident in 1980.'

'This is like an episode of the *X Files*.'

'It is, but we're onto something here.'

'Are you *sure* the symbols are the same?'

'There are some minor discrepancies, but that's not too surprising in the circumstances. I'd say they're the same.'

'And you read all this on the internet?'

'The story is tucked away on a website run by the *UFO Truth Society*. Hold on a minute and I'll find their details … let's see … here we are … there's a list of contact names, and one of them is based in Liverpool.'

'But what more could you learn by talking to them?'

'Maybe nothing, but it's worth a try.'

'Tread carefully,' Vine said. 'If the symbols *are* a match, Hartford was telling the truth, and we're moving into dangerous territory.'

'I'll just say I'm into UFOs and want to know more about this particular incident.'

The door handle turned.

'Ron, I have to go. Let me know how it goes with Joyce.'

Jan popped her head around. 'How long are you going to be?'

Colin shut the laptop. 'Just finished.'

Chapter Twenty-three

Friday, 27th March

Colin closed his office door and dialled the mobile number.

'Hello?'

'Is that Geoff Maloney?'

'Yes, it is. Who's this?'

His accent was reminiscent of a young Paul McCartney.

'My name's Colin Thurcroft. I've been looking at your website, and the Cascade UFO crash caught my attention.'

'It's a good read, isn't it?'

'Just a bit.'

'Pity none of it can be corroborated.'

'Even the Kleins?'

'Bill Klein did go missing, and his daughter died in a car accident after kicking up a fuss, but we're still a long way from proving anything.'

'So everything you know is on the site?'

'Not exactly.'

'Why's that?'

'Can you tell me a bit more about yourself and why you're interested in this case?'

'Yeah … I'm thirty-nine, married with one child, and I employ twenty-six people to supply hiking gear through the internet. I've been interested in the paranormal since I was a kid, but I've only just got into UFOs, especially the crash retrievals.' Colin scanned the printout on his desk. 'I've studied the well-known cases, but I've come to the conclusion that, if there is any truth to this, it may well be hiding in the more obscure stuff.'

Silence.

'Hello?'

'Whereabouts are you?'

'Cranshaw.'

'Can you get into Liverpool tomorrow? About two o'clock?'

'Err … yeah … I suppose so.'

'Sorry if it all sounds a bit cloak and dagger, but it's not something I want to discuss over the phone. It'll make more sense when we've had a face to face chat.'

'It's your call, Geoff.'

'I'll text the address to you.'

'Okay.'

'And bring some identification.'

'No problem.'

'See you tomorrow.'

'Bye.'

Colin stared out at the car park. 'Identification?'

When the address arrived, he opened up Google Earth and typed in the post code.

Chapter Twenty-four

'Barmaid said the food's on its way.' Colin placed the drinks on the table and sat down. 'I forgot to tell you I'll be working most of tomorrow.'

Jan sipped her gin and tonic. 'How come?'

'The shop has set things back, and I need to catch up on paperwork.'

'Is that all?'

'Sorry?'

'Since when have *you* been interested in UFOs?'

'Holly caught me sketching some new logo designs and – '

'I know, Col, she told me, but I'm not *twelve*.'

'What's that supposed to mean?'

'You're up to something, aren't you?'

A flush of heat climbed his neck. 'Like what?'

'Chasing a dead man's crazy idea.'

'I'm following up a few leads, that's all.'

'Leads? You're a detective now, are you?'

He sighed. 'I wasn't going to say anything until I'd had chance to look into it properly – the thing is I've been approached by an old friend of Eric Manning's.'

'When was this?'

'Wednesday, at the funeral.'

'You gate-crashed his funeral?'

'I wouldn't say *gate-crashed*, but I wanted to pay my respects.'

She rolled her eyes. 'Unbelievable … '

'This friend of his said the weird hat allowed Eric to leave his body and see the past. He used to stay with him when he did it, but, this one time he didn't wake up. He tried to help him, but he wouldn't eat or drink and died a few weeks later.'

'And he didn't think to call an ambulance?'

'It wouldn't have done any good.'

'For who?

'He had to return to his body in *that* room, Jan. Rushing him to a hospital would've only made matters worse.'

She shook her head. 'You need to tell the police.'

'He's in his late seventies. What good would it do now?'

'You're withholding information.'

'Maybe, but this isn't a murder enquiry.'

'Did *he* take the bank books?'

He nodded and took a mouthful of beer.

Jan fixed him with a hard stare. 'Jesus Christ, Col.'

'He was scared, Jan. He knew the police wouldn't believe him.'

'You don't say?'

'The case went cold forty years ago. Opening up to me isn't the behaviour of a man who'd effectively got away with murder.'

She shrugged. 'So what does he gain from telling you?'

'He wanted to warn me.'

'About what?'

'Eric encountered something when he was out of body; something very sinister that wanted to cross into our world.'

Jan snorted. 'So the bogeyman killed him?'

'Sort of.'

'And he flies around in a UFO, does he?'

'There's a match between the symbols Holly saw in the documentary and something Eric described.'

She studied her drink.

'Please, Jan – just bear with me for a little while.'

'You've put me in an impossible situation.'

'How's that?'

'If you get mixed up in a murder, where does that leave me and Holly?'

'You're overreacting.'

'Am I?'

His response was stymied when a waitress arrived with their meals.

Chapter Twenty-five

'You've had another row?' Holly said. 'I *know* you have.'

'Finish your breakfast,' Colin said.

'You slept in the spare room and Mum's still in bed.'

'Nice work, Chief Wiggum.'

She pulled a face and took her cereal bowl to the sink.

'What're you up to today?' he said.

'Going into town with Kirsty and Nicola.'

He took a ten pound note from his wallet. 'Don't spend it on rubbish.'

She reached across the table and slid it from his fingers. 'Thanks, Dad.'

The assured commands from the sat nav brought Colin to within half a mile of the city centre. He found the charity shop without fuss, but it took another five minutes to sniff out a parking space within reasonable walking distance.

The door to the upstairs flat was tucked away down a narrow, dank passageway.

He pressed the intercom button and waited.

'Hello?'

'Hello, it's Colin Thurcroft for Geoff Maloney.'

'Be right down.'

The hollow rumble of footsteps came to an abrupt halt when the door was opened by a man no older than forty in faded jeans and a black t-shirt. Shoulder length, lank, brown hair framed a high forehead, and hooded grey eyes met his through thin designer glasses.

Colin smiled awkwardly and held out his driving license.

He glanced at it and nodded his approval. 'Come on up.'

At the top of the steep stairs, a galley kitchen opened onto a spacious lounge lit by the wide front window. The aroma of cooked bacon lingered in the warm air.

'Make yourself at home,' Geoff said. 'What would you like to drink?'

Colin removed his jacket. 'I'm fine thanks.'

'Just me then,' he said and returned to the kitchen.

Colin sat down in a black leather Poäng chair and surveyed the room.

The low sofa was strewn with magazines. Along the far wall, a wide monitor sat on a glass and steel desk crammed with several PCs wreathed in a bird's nest of cables. A compact hi-fi system fought for space in a stylish book cabinet. Framed posters of classic science fiction movies crowded the pastel blue walls.

Geoff returned with a bottle of Becks and cleared a space on the sofa.

He sat down and raised the bottle to Colin. 'Sure you won't join me?'

Colin smiled. 'I would if I wasn't driving.'

'Right then,' Geoff said. 'The Cascade Crash. You want to know why I wouldn't discuss it over the phone.'

'That's why I'm here.'

'There's been a development with this case that we deemed too sensitive for the website, and I wanted to meet you face to face before saying anything else.'

Colin nodded. 'That's fair enough.'

'First things first: do you have any ties with other groups?'

'You mean UFOs, yeah?'

Geoff nodded.

'No, you're the first one I've approached. Like I said, I have a hunch that the truth is buried in discredited information. The Cascade Crash is a fascinating case, and I'd like to find out more about it. You could call me an enthusiastic amateur without causing offence.'

Geoff smiled.

Colin held out his hands. 'I'll join *your* group if it helps.'

'It's okay, la; I'm not on a recruitment drive.' Geoff leaned back and crossed his legs. 'A couple of years ago, we were approached by a woman who claimed to be the daughter of the whistle blower who made contact with Klein.' He took a swig of beer. 'Me and a colleague went down to Devon to meet her. She said she was born in California, but her mum died in childbirth, and she moved here with her father when she was three-years-old. Apparently, he never went back to see friends or family and always seemed evasive when asked about his life before the move. She said she'd made contact because of a conversation at his funeral a few months earlier. Apparently, she'd got talking to his closest friend about his reticence to discuss the past, and he described an incident that still troubled him. Allegedly, a good few years back, they were at a works Christmas party when a local UFO sighting was mentioned, and the banter drifted to the subject in general. They were all pretty drunk, and someone got quite vocal about how ridiculous it all was. Her father didn't agree and things got heated, so his friend took him outside to calm down. When he asked why he'd reacted like that, he said he'd worked on a crashed UFO at a top secret location and had seen the alien crew.' Geoff took another swig. 'He thought the world had a right to know and approached Klein soon after his book was published. They met up at a disused gas stop in Nevada, but, the next day, he received an anonymous tip off that his cover was blown. He drove his daughter to a safe house, organised changes of identity and fled the country. He managed to warn Bill Klein but didn't know if he'd got away. Anyway, the next day, her dad denied everything and blamed it on the drink. They never spoke about it again, but the friend suspected no smoke without fire and made notes of what he'd divulged. When he died, he decided to tell his daughter.'

'What did she want from you?'

'Fifty grand to tell us about the little green men.'

Colin frowned. 'Sounds like Seth Hartford all over again.'

Geoff nodded. 'I actually said that to her, but she claimed it was insurance for when the story broke and the shit hit the fan. Anyway, we agreed to go back and brief the rest of the group. I proposed that we offer an interim payment while her claims were investigated. Unfortunately, I was outvoted nine to three.'

'Why were they so against what could be the biggest story ever?'

'Serious researchers wouldn't touch the Cascade Crash with a barge pole. We have limited funds, and she was asking crazy money for little more than drunken hearsay at best.'

Colin leaned forward. 'I'd like to meet her.'

'She's contacted other paranormal groups, wanting the same amount.'

'I can afford it,' Colin said.

Geoff narrowed his eyes. 'I think you should cut to the chase.'

'Sorry?'

'I don't think you've been entirely honest with me.'

Colin sighed. 'I have access to information that corroborates Seth Hartford's story.'

'Let's hear it.'

'Sorry, Geoff, I can't say any more than that.'

'Why not?'

'It's nothing sinister, but I want to keep a lid on it until I have all the facts.'

'Seems like one way traffic to me.'

Colin nodded. 'I know it must seem that way.'

'Too right it does.'

'Look – I think you've given me just enough to track her down, but it'd be a lot easier with an introduction from you.'

Geoff twirled the bottle and drained it in two gulps. 'I need another one.'

The thought occurred to Colin that his intake of alcohol could go either way, and he offered a silent prayer that it would have a persuasive effect.

Geoff returned with a beer and sat down. 'Is there *any* way I can get in on this?'

Colin shook his head. 'I have to go it alone for now.'

'I can bring a lot to the table.'

'I'm sure you can, and you're first on the list if I do need help.'

'We don't have to involve the society.'

'I'll bear it in mind.'

An awkward silence ensued, which Colin was determined not to break.

Come on, Geoffrey. You know you want to ...

Geoff took a swig. 'Okay – she calls herself Carol Glenister, which I very much doubt is her real name. She said they came here in 1973, so she'll be … forty-four this year – '

Colin pulled a small notebook and pen from his jacket.

' – I'd say she's around five-five, slim build, not bad looking, long black hair which I suspect was dyed – and she was dressed a bit butch, if you know what I mean like.'

'And she lives in Devon?'

'From her accent, I'd say she was native.'

'Address?'

'We didn't meet at her home. She told us to set out from Woolacombe at a specific time and follow the coastal path towards Ilfracombe. She had a detailed description of us, but we didn't have a clue about her. She could've strolled by without giving herself away if she didn't like what she saw.'

'Not a bad plan.'

'She's not daft, I'll say that much.'

'So you met in the open air?'

'About three miles from Woolacombe. It was a nice day, but we were cream crackered; that path is all up hill and down dale. After the meeting, we had to give her a ten minute start – I think she headed inland but couldn't say for sure.'

'Do you have a phone number?'

Geoff shook his head. 'She called us, number withheld.'

'Didn't take any chances, did she?'

'Like I said, she's not daft, but I got the impression she knew that path like the back of her hand – I suppose, if you hung around long enough, you'd bump into her.'

'Anything else I should know?'

'Just that she had a dog with her: a black Labrador bitch.'

Colin closed his notebook. 'Thanks for this, Geoff.'

'I hope you find what you're looking for.'

He smiled. 'If nothing else, the sea air will do me good.'

In the passageway, Colin thanked him again and held out his hand.

Geoff ignored it. 'I've just remembered what I meant to ask you.'

Colin dropped his arm. 'Go on.'

'Are you from Cranshaw originally?'

He smiled. 'For my sins. Why?'

'Do you know about the UFO sighting there in 1975?'

He frowned and shook his head. 'First I've heard, to be honest.'

'It *was* a long time ago. I just wondered if you knew anybody who'd seen it. We're always on the lookout for fresh evidence.'

'What exactly happened?'

'In the early hours of October the twenty-third, a number of people witnessed two bright blue orbs over the town. After about ten minutes, they shot upwards at an unbelievable speed and disappeared.'

Colin swallowed hard. 'It's a new one on me.'

'The story got buried because of a bad fire at a local factory the same night.'

'Atkins and Sons.'

'That's the one. Anyway, we tracked down a retired flight controller who worked at Manchester Airport at the time, and he confirmed that two unidentified objects *were* logged that night around twenty miles west of the airport.'

He tried a thoughtful expression. 'I'll have to ask my mum about it.'

'Worth a go,' Geoff said. 'Let me know if you come up with anything.'

'I will.'

'And keep me posted about the other thing.'

Colin held out his hand. 'I'll do my best.'

'You know where I am if you need me.'

They shook briefly.

He turned to go. 'Bye, Geoff, and thanks again.'

'Good luck, la.'

The door slam reverberated along the passageway.

Chapter Twenty-six

Colin's imagination slipped effortlessly into overdrive. He tried to reel it in, but the UFO sighting and the factory fire were too much of a coincidence. He was only yards from the car when his phone rang and chased away the glowing orbs. The number was unfamiliar.

'Hello?'

'Hello, could I speak to Mr Colin Thurcroft?'

'Speaking.'

'Mr Thurcroft, this is Detective Inspector Brian Taylor. I'm heading up the inquiry into the sudden death at the property you recently purchased.'

'What can I do for you?'

'I need your help with a couple of things.'

'Go on.'

'Can you come down to Cranshaw police station?'

'Today?'

'The sooner the better.'

'I'm in Liverpool at the moment, but I'll get there as soon as I can.'

'Ask for me at the front desk.'

'Okay – bye.'

'Bye for now.'

Colin introduced himself to the desk sergeant, and then surveyed his seating options on the row of mismatched plastic chairs. To his left: a scrawny, vividly-tattooed youth in a tight vest and scruffy tracksuit bottoms; hunched forward and staring at the floor. To his right: a fleshy, lank-haired woman, who looked fifty but was probably not much older than thirty, in a short denim skirt and pink jacket; eyes closed, hands under her thighs, rocking gently to and fro.

He sat down between them and crossed his legs.

The smell of ripe sweat and stale alcohol found his nostrils, but he couldn't decide which of them it was coming from. He took shallow breaths and stared straight ahead in the hope neither would try and strike up a conversation.

The minutes ticked by, and the smell got worse.

He heard a dull clunk and the whine of hinges over to his right, but his eyes remained fixed on the clock above the front desk.

A moment later, a jaded male voice called his name.

Thank fuck!

DI Taylor was a thickset man with a shaved head and a face only a mother could love. His casual attire suggested this wasn't his shift.

After a curt greeting and perfunctory handshake, he led Colin to a windowless room at the end of a long corridor.

'I thought you said this wasn't a formal interview.'

Taylor gestured towards the steel table and chairs. 'It isn't.'

Colin sat down and unzipped his jacket.

Taylor sat opposite and folded his arms. 'Thanks for coming in, Mr Thurcroft. I know neither of us wants to be here, but there's been a development that won't keep 'til Monday.'

'Development?'

'We took a call from your wife this morning, claiming that Mr Manning had been murdered by someone of your recent acquaintance.'

Colin shut his eyes and clenched his teeth.

Fuck's sake, Jan ...

'Less than an hour later, an elderly gentleman arrived with a note from Mr Manning's sister requesting the release of the device that was on his head. He said he'd been a close friend of the deceased but wouldn't give a reason why he wanted it. I decided to ask him a few questions and wasn't entirely satisfied with his response. In consequence, he's been released on the understanding he'll be questioned further, probably under caution.'

'He's not a murderer.'

'Who isn't?'

'Ronald Vine.'

'So we *are* talking about the same person.'

'It would seem so.'

'I'm told you met at the funeral, where he disclosed a strange story about Mr Manning's out of body activities.'

'That's right, but I didn't take it too seriously.'

'Your wife said Mr Vine stole Mr Manning's bank books.'

Colin sighed. 'Jan has been uneasy ever since we found the body. When I told her about Ron, she put two and two together and got six.'

'According to her, he was there when Mr Manning died.'

'I wouldn't know about that.'

'Come on, Mr Thurcroft. Are you saying she's making that up as well?'

'I don't know what she's playing at to be honest, other than wasting police time.'

'If you're trying to protect Mr Vine, you could – '

'I'm not, and this is starting to feel like a formal interview.'

Taylor sighed and glanced at his watch. 'Okay, we'll leave it there for now, but expect a call from me in the not too distant future.'

Colin banged on the dirty glass and squinted into the room. Nothing seemed out of place. The only thing that caught his attention was an empty vodka bottle on the coffee table.

He returned to the front door and opened the letterbox. 'Ron! It's Colin!'

He could see Ronald Vine's scuffed brogues about ten feet away.

'Come on, mate, open the door … '

Something wasn't right.

They were pointing down like a ballerina.

Six inches above the floor.

Colin turned away when the body bag was stretchered into the ambulance. He sat down on the neighbour's front wall and took a few deep breaths.

A dark blue Audi A6 came to a halt across the street.

DI Taylor got out of the front passenger door and strolled towards him.

He stopped a few feet away and lit a cigarette. 'Must've been quite a shock.'

'You could say that.'

He blew smoke from his nostrils. 'Anything you want to tell me?'

'I hardly knew him, but he seemed like a decent man to me.'

'Not somebody who'd commit murder?'

'I don't know what to think anymore.'

Taylor sniffed and walked away. 'Like I said, I'll be in touch.'

Chapter Twenty-seven

Sunday, 30th March, 11.12am

Colin placed the rucksack next to the sports bag and stared at the smashed mug in the sink. The scattered shards could've been a metaphor for his marriage: broken, all but impossible to repair and hazardous to even try.

Jan strode into the kitchen and poured herself some more wine.

He looked on impassively.

She'd started to dye her long auburn hair a few years ago, and the crow's feet were visible before she smiled. But she could still turn heads when she tried, and Holly's difficult pregnancy hadn't swelled her slender figure in the slightest. The physical attraction was still strong but tempered by the unalterable fact that, when the whirlwind of their courtship had eventually blown itself out, two quite different people with different needs had been left in its wake.

She took a quick sip and met his gaze. 'Well?'

'I'll give you a call in a week or so.'

'Whatever.'

'I know it's a cliché, but we both need some space.'

'It's a cop out, that's what it is.'

'You didn't trust me, and a man's dead because of it.'

'How many times do I have to say it? I never meant for *that* to happen.'

'Save it, Jan – I'm not in the mood.'

She returned to the lounge. 'Neither am I, so why don't you just jog on.'

The daylight was fading fast when Colin knocked on the guesthouse door. A genial young woman checked him in and carried his rucksack to the first floor, en suite room. The tired, chintzy décor recalled childhood holidays, but everything was spotlessly clean.

'Have you been to Ilfracombe before?'

'No, this is my first time.'

'It's quiet this time of year, but you'll see other walkers on the coastal paths.'

He dropped the sports bag onto the bed. 'I hope so.'

Part Three

Over the hills and far away

Chapter Twenty-eight

Next morning, Colin skipped breakfast and headed into town. He bought an OS map, bottled water and sandwiches, and then made his way to the twin, grey-brick funnels which crowned the Landmark Theatre. He found a bench, overlooking the rocky bay below Capstone Hill, and pulled out his phone to compose an email.

Hi Alan,

I'll be conspicuous by my absence this morning.

No easy way to say it but I've decided to take some time off on my own.

You know things haven't been good between Jan and me for some time, so I can't imagine it's come as much of a shock.

Not sure what the future holds other than I won't let it compromise the business.

In the meantime, I'd like you to take the reins. I'm sure you and Kath can run the show for a week or two, and I promise to make it worth your while.

I'm chillaxing (sort of) in Devon at the moment but give me a call anytime if you want to talk (business or otherwise).

Cheers,

Col

He sent it, and then phoned Holly.

'Hi Dad.'

'Can you talk?'

'Yeah, it's break time.'

'How's things?'

'What do you think?'

He swallowed hard. 'Sorry we didn't get chance to have a proper talk yesterday.'

'It's okay.'

'No, it's not, but things got out of hand, as you know.'

'Where are you?'

'Devon.'

'Where's that?'

'Good God, Holly! Don't they teach you anything these days?'

'It's down south, isn't it?'

'Yeah, close enough.'

'I don't want you and Mum to split up.'

'I know you don't, and we might not. But I meant what I said yesterday: whatever happens, I'll always be there for you.'

'When're you coming back?'

'In a week or two, maybe sooner.'

'You'll miss parents' day.'

He winced. 'Sorry, Love, it slipped my mind.'

'No biggie.'

An awkward silence ensued, and he fought to control his emotions.

'I have to go now, Holly, but I'll stay in touch, okay?'

'Love you.'

'Love you too … '

'Bye, Dad.'

'Bye, Hol.'

Colin ended the call and took a deep breath.

He managed to smile at an elderly couple, and then reached for his rucksack.

Chapter Twenty-nine

Thursday, 3rd April

When he reached the steep, winding descent to the narrow bay, Colin sat down on the wooden bench and watched a distant container ship slog up the Bristol Channel. It was his fourth day on the coastal path after another night of cheap wine and humdrum television in his room. Desperate internet research hadn't produced any leads worth chasing up, and his earlier optimism was ebbing away.

The sun took a cautious peek through the swathes of rain clouds.

He unzipped his jacket and closed his eyes.

The gentle sea breeze caressed his skin.

Tangled thoughts began to unwind …

He woke with a start when something struck his chest.

A Border Collie sniffed his face, and then ran off into the long grass.

He surveyed the path but saw no one within half a mile. He got to his feet and looked down into the bay. Ten feet below, the sea breeze teased a mane of jet-black hair.

He returned to the bench and sat down.

The woman reached the top and stopped to get her breath back.

She was dressed in a faded denim jacket, camouflage combat trousers and leather boots; and appeared to be the right age and height.

The dog ran towards her, and she ruffled its fur.

'Hello,' he said. 'Enjoying the walk?'

Jesus H! That sounded naff!

She looked up and smiled warmly. 'That climb felt steeper than ever today, but it's cheaper than joining a gym.'

Her gentle West Country accent was further confirmation, but the dog was wrong.

He returned the smile. 'I know what you mean.'

She followed the barking dog as it bounded off along the path.

His heart was beating fast now.

He stood up and cleared his throat. 'I hope you don't mind me asking – '

She stopped and turned around.

'You wouldn't be Carol Glenister, by any chance?'

She frowned and shook her head. 'Are you looking for her?'

'Yes, I am, and you fit the description – apart from the dog that is – I was told she walks a black Labrador along here.'

'She wouldn't be the only one.'

He sighed. 'Thought as much.'

'Best of luck,' she said flatly and walked away.

'Sorry to have bothered you … '

Colin watched her for the best part of a minute.

He wondered if she'd turn around, but she didn't.

He sat down and ran his fingers through his tousled hair.

There was another container ship on the horizon.

It was heading out to sea, and, just for a moment, he wished he was on it.

Chapter Thirty

Friday, 4th April

'The plate is very hot,' the young Polish waitress said.

Colin surveyed the generous cooked breakfast.

'Would you like some more toast?'

'No, I'm fine thanks.'

'Enjoy your breakfast,' she said and headed back to the kitchen.

He'd made it to the dining room just before the nine o'clock cut off. Now he was alone at the table next to the front window.

He sliced off the end of a thick pork sausage and dipped it into an egg yolk. As he chewed, he gazed at the quiet street and mulled over the possibility of widening the search area, but the rivulets of rain on the glass taunted his dwindling enthusiasm.

He was buttering a slice of toast when the proprietor approached.

'Sorry to interrupt, Mr Thurcroft,' she said. 'But there's somebody to see you.'

'I wasn't expecting anyone.'

'She wouldn't give a name, but she said you'd want to speak to her.'

'Can she come through?'

'Of course.'

She left the dining room.

A moment later, the woman from the coastal path appeared in the doorway.

She strode towards his table and sat down.

'I'll get straight to the point,' she said. 'Who are you and what do you want?'

'You don't stand on ceremony, do you?'

She fixed him with a hard stare.

'Okay, we'll play it your way. My name's Colin Thurcroft. I'm a business owner from Lancashire who wants to know more about the Cascade crash.'

'What type of business?'

'I sell hiking gear on the internet.'

'And how did you find out about me?'

'I approached the UFO Truth Society, and they told me what they knew.'

'What draws a clothing retailer to that particular case?'

'That's for me to know.'

She leaned back and folded her arms. 'Wrong answer.'

'Would fifty grand get me off the hook?'

'It might.'

'Cheque or banker's draft?'

She stifled a smile and plucked a piece of toast from the rack.

The rain had stopped when they left the guesthouse.

She set off down the street with a purposeful stride. 'Fancy a walk to the harbour?'

Colin glanced at the slate grey sky and zipped his jacket. 'Do I have a choice?'

They'd gone at least three hundred yards before she spoke again.

'How long have you been looking for me?'

'This is the fifth day.'

'Did you suspect I was lying yesterday?'

He shrugged. 'I did wonder, but the dog threw me off.'

'Poppy died six months ago – I couldn't get another black Lab; it was too painful.'

'Collies are real livewires aren't they?'

'Tell me about it.'

'Can't have been easy following me.'

She smiled. 'I kept him on a tight lead.'

'So when I returned to a humble guesthouse, you knew I wasn't CIA.'

'More than likely, but you're not in the clear *just* yet.'

They walked in silence again until they reached the quay.

She gazed up, with undisguised disdain, at the towering bronze statue of a naked, pregnant woman standing on a pile of books with a raised sword in one hand and a set of scales held under her buttocks in the other. The flesh on her right side had been peeled and incised to display the underlying musculature, bone and foetus.

'Damien Hirst, yeah?' he said.

She nodded. 'Hideous, isn't it?'

'An acquired taste.'

'We should count our blessings it's not the real thing in a vat of formaldehyde.'

She strolled to the edge of the quay and folded her arms on the railings above the foaming green waves.

Colin joined her. 'Do you live in Ilfracombe?'

'Let's talk some more about you.'

'Fire away.'

'You see, nobody has ever taken me seriously. Then, right out of the blue, you turn up waving a cheque book.'

'Happy days.'

'No doubt, but what's the catch?'

'I've seen the five symbols before, but they weren't on a crashed UFO.'

'Tell me more.'

He watched two herring gulls in a noisy mid-air duel. 'That's all I'm prepared to say.'

'Looks like we're at stalemate,' she said. 'But there *is* an alternative.'

'Go on.'

'Forget the money. You show me yours, and I'll show you mine.'

'Sorry?'

'I want to know what you know.'

Colin stared into her dark green eyes. 'A man's dead because of what *I* know.'

'Are you trying to frighten me?'

'I'm trying to impress on you just how serious this is.'

'How did he die?'

'Hung himself five days ago.'

'Why?'

'I've said too much already.'

She looked out to sea. 'What did the UFO geeks tell you?'

'That your father worked on the Oregon craft and blew the whistle to Bill Klein, that he brought you here when his cover was blown, and he only ever talked about it to a friend after a drunken row at a Christmas party.'

She frowned. 'Not a bad summary.'

'Apparently, you held back about the alien crew for the fifty k.'

'So you're no further forward than they are.'

'Except *I* have the money.'

'And something far more valuable to me.' She turned towards him. 'You're the first person I've met who could corroborate Dad's story.'

'I was told you wanted the dosh to do a runner?'

'There's a bit more to it than that. The money was both bait *and* insurance. I reasoned that anybody who'd stump up that amount would pull out all the stops to get the truth, but it was there for me if things got out of hand.'

Colin chewed his lip. 'What's to stop you walking away after I've spilled?'

'Because I'll go first.'

'Okay,' he said. 'The floor's yours.'

She took a deep breath. 'All five of the crew survived the crash and were alive and well when Dad was recruited in the sixties. He called them *Polyforms* because they could morph into any shape to satisfy the requirements of a part organic brain about twice the size of ours. They were telepathic and easy to communicate with, but their technology was incomprehensible, and little, if any, reverse engineering was accomplished.'

'Anything else?'

'Not about the crew,' she said. 'Don't forget this was a drunken confession relayed to me, second hand, many years later.'

'Fair enough, but I was expecting a bit more bang for bucks, to be honest.'

'Hold your horses. The last thing he said won't disappoint.' She glanced around the quayside. 'In 1963, an identical craft crashed in the UK.'

'Whereabouts?'

'The Scottish highlands. It was retrieved and taken to a top secret facility not far from your neck of the woods.'

He narrowed his eyes. 'How far?'

'Do you know the Lake District?'

'Better than most.'

'Dad said it's under a hill near Thirlmere.'

A broad smile creased Colin's face. 'That's the money shot.'

Chapter Thirty-one

'Worth every penny,' Wendy said. 'And you got it for free.'

'Did he say which hill?'

She shook her heard.

'Were the crew still alive?'

She shrugged. 'I've told you all I know.'

'Don't take this the wrong way, but I need to ask – '

'About Dad?'

Colin nodded. 'Any doubts?'

'None whatsoever,' she said. 'He was the antithesis of a Walter Mitty, highly intelligent, honest to a fault and very down to earth. This story is so out of character it has to be true, and the man that told me was like an uncle to me.'

'And there's me thinking all the crashed UFOs are stored at Area 51.'

'Apparently not.'

'Do you have *anything* to back this up?'

'I've spent weeks up there in fruitless searches for hard evidence.'

'What did you expect? Secret base next left after the cattle grid?'

She cuffed his arm. 'I wore out a good pair of boots traipsing those hills.'

He winked. 'I can get you discount on a new pair.'

'Thanks,' she said. 'I'll hold you to that.'

'So there's nothing to go on?'

'Not quite,' she said. 'I always stayed at the King's Head on the eastern side of the reservoir. One evening, I got chatting to an old farmer and asked him about local folklore. I got the usual bollocks about ghosts and goblins, but then he mentioned what he called *goings on* around the reservoir. He couldn't remember the exact year, but he said that in the early-sixties, for a period of several months, the water board shut the road along the western shoreline, and walkers were prevented from crossing the nearby hills. The official explanation was overdue maintenance to the overflow system and aqueduct. But people started to ask questions when explosions and low flying helicopters were heard at night, and a group of walkers got into fisticuffs with some security men. He said things did return to normal, but nocturnal helicopters are still heard in the area.'

'The timing's right,' Colin said. 'But the water board's explanation is credible, especially if they were using explosives to shift rock. And the helicopters could be on military exercise; you do see fighter jets hugging the valleys up there.'

'Fair comment, but I heard two more tales that might convince you otherwise.'

'Go on.'

'He said that, about fifteen years ago, a young couple arrived at the pub with a strange story to tell. They'd just hiked over from Derwent Water. Somewhere near Raven Crag, they got caught in a squall and sheltered in the woods. It took a while to clear, but, as they were about to break cover, a black helicopter passed very low overhead and landed on a rocky outcrop. The two men and a woman that got out were dressed for the outdoors but carrying attaché cases. The helicopter lifted off and headed south, and the passengers ran into the trees. The couple went up to the outcrop and searched the area, but there was no sign of them or any clues as to why they were there.'

'That's worth looking into,' he said.

'Problem is: I've retraced their route from both directions without finding a rock you'd want to land a helicopter on.'

'I wouldn't be too despondent. They may've misjudged their location; it's easy to do up there in bad weather.'

'Tell me about it.'

'So what else did the farmer divulge?'

'He didn't, but another drinker chipped in with this one: United Utilities own and maintain the reservoir. Around ten years ago, he was driving along the western shore late at night when one of their Land Rovers pulled out from a dirt track. He swerved to avoid it and scraped his front wing on a stone wall. To his surprise, the driver was a middle-aged American woman in a smart business suit. Rather than swap insurance details, she asked him which garage would best repair the car. He mentioned Cumbria Motors in Keswick, and she told him to take it there and everything would be taken care of. The next day, he did exactly that, and a mechanic said a credit card number had been phoned through and gave him the keys to a courtesy car with a full tank of petrol.'

'Interesting story,' Colin said. 'But there could – '

'Hold on.' She wagged a finger. 'The garage closed down a few years ago, and I couldn't find an ex-employee to corroborate the story, but I phoned United Utilities and was told that everything goes through their insurance, and a quick fix at a local garage was a serious breach of company policy. The person I spoke to was genuinely puzzled when I described the driver and the time of the accident. He actually said that whoever'd told me this was mistaken or pulling my leg.'

'Do you think he might've been?'

She shrugged. 'You never know, but he seemed sincere to me. They both did.'

'Have you told anybody else about this?'

'Not a soul,' she said. 'And now it's your turn.'

Colin nodded. 'Brace yourself for a bumpy ride. It all started when I bought a disused building to convert into a retail outlet … '

He recounted everything that'd happened from the discovery of Eric Manning's body to the bust up with Jan. She frowned and narrowed her eyes on several occasions, but she only interrupted to request more information about the machine Eric built and the UFO incident over Cranshaw.

When he'd finished, he turned to the sea. 'And that, as they say, is that.'

'Good God,' she said. 'I'm speechless … '

'I wouldn't be offended if you doubted my sanity.'

'No, I believe you. Really, I do.'

They didn't speak for nearly a minute.

'So,' she said. 'Where do we go from here?'

He blew out his cheeks. 'Don't know, to be honest. I feel like I'm standing at a crossroads. If I take the safe path, I can get on with my life and maybe even salvage my marriage. God only knows where the other one will take me.'

'I thought you wanted some answers.'

'I do, but I'm starting to appreciate the scale of this thing. You could spend a lifetime chasing your own tail, or make a breakthrough and get bundled into a car by men in black.'

'I wouldn't disagree,' she said. 'It's a decision only you can make.'

'A decision that could potentially put my wife and daughter in the firing line and ruin my business. I assume there would be similar repercussions for you.'

She shrugged. 'Self-employed, parents gone and divorced for nearly six years. I wanted kids but couldn't take one to term. When my body waved the white flag, he left to sow his seed in more fertile ground. I haven't dated seriously since.'

'Sorry – I didn't mean to pry.'

'Don't worry, you didn't.'

He tried a sympathetic smile. 'Do *you* want to take this further?'

'In all honesty, I'd just about given up, but you've put the fire back in my belly.'

'Glad to be of service.'

'And I'm very grateful, but there is *one* more thing you could do.'

'Go on.'

'Your shopkeeper and my father experienced the same alien technology, yeah?'

He nodded.

'Before you make a decision, let's kick it around and see if anything sticks.'

He frowned. 'Can't see any harm in that.'

'I live twenty minutes away, and there's enough in the fridge for lunch.'

'In that case, dinner tonight is on me.'

Where did that come from?

'Okay.' She smiled warmly. 'It's a deal.'

'Is this the point where you tell me your real name?'

She winked. 'No flies on you, are there?'

'Didn't take much to work *that* one out.'

'My name's Wendy Cooper, or at least it has been since I left the states. I suppose I'll never know what I was called at birth.'

He held out his hand. 'Nice to meet you, Wendy.'

She shook it and smiled. 'And you, Colin.'

Wendy took him around the harbour and up a steep, tree-bordered lane towards the main road into town. Here, they turned left and headed into the quiet suburbs.

Colin told her more than he expected to about his personal life and business, and she talked candidly about her divorce and the patchy fortunes of a freelance interior designer.

By the time they reached the row of cream-brick terraced houses, he felt like he'd known her for years. But there was something else in the mix: a strong attraction he hadn't experienced since meeting Jan nearly twenty years ago. It was a pleasant surprise and a complication he could do without. His marriage was a slow motion train wreck, but he still had feelings for Jan, and Holly was his life. He'd no idea if Wendy felt anything beyond the platonic, and their nascent friendship could be ruined by a clumsy pass over a good meal and several glasses of wine.

Am I on the rebound already?

'Chez moi,' she said and climbed the steps to the arched front door.

In the hallway, she made a fuss of the exuberant dog and gestured at a distressed pine door. 'Go through and make yourself at home. I'll feed Toby and get the kettle on.'

The living room was more or less as he expected. Tall, potted plants and a red velvet suite enclosed a Persian rug in front of a marble fireplace. Framed, vintage posters of psychic events hung low on voguish, floral wallpaper.

Colin studied the stylish illustrations of crystal balls, black cats and tarot cards; and made a mental note to ask her about them later.

He got comfortable in an armchair and let his thoughts drift.

When Wendy entered with a tinkling tea tray, he was roaming the bleak fells above Thirlmere.

She set it on a low table and plonked herself down on the sofa. 'Milk and sugar?'

'Just milk thanks.'

Toby jumped onto the sofa and nuzzled up to her.

She poured the tea. 'Where do you want to start?'

'Not sure,' he said. 'But something's just occurred to me.'

'What's that?'

'These aliens are a bit accident prone, aren't they?'

'They seem to be, but there has to be more to it than pilot error.'

'Like what?'

She passed him a mug. 'Don't know, but it's hard to believe they could navigate the vast tracts of interstellar space with technology that baffled our best minds, and then go tits up when they got here.'

'Good point.'

'And, despite the fact both events *actually* happened, the Scottish crash is unknown to the UFO community, and Seth Hartford has been written off as a hoaxer.'

'Now there's an irony.'

'A massive one, in my opinion. Government endorsed disinformation is nothing new, and it's highly likely the more well-known UFO crashes are a smokescreen for these two.'

He smiled. 'That was my opening gambit with Geoff Maloney.'

'A while ago, I watched a documentary about stealth technology. Some alleged military experts were interviewed, and they said the US Air Force and secret services were more than happy to let the public mistake top secret aircraft for flying saucers. Better that than give the game away to the Russians.'

He sipped his tea. 'Not a bad strategy.'

They didn't speak for a few moments.

Wendy broke the silence. 'I can hear your cogs turning from here.'

'I bet you can – the way I see it, these Polyforms must've made telepathic contact with Eric from inside one of the spheres, which means they projected a human form to appeal to him, and then lied about the teleportation cock up.'

She nodded. 'And poor Eric fell for it hook, line and sinker.'

'Rod, reel and bait box, but Ron destroyed his machine, so they must've got to Roger Atkins when he tried out the other one.'

'The UFO sighting over Cranshaw is the clincher.'

'Absolutely,' he said. 'Two downed spheres held in secret bases; doorways through space created by machines designed by their crews; and then the grand finale: two glowing orbs hovering over the melted prototype shop that made said machines.'

'It's all falling into place, isn't it?'

'The events certainly are, but the reasoning behind it is puzzling.'

'Go on.'

'Why employ such a long-winded and destructive procedure? Why not just leave the bases and fly away without all the drama?'

'Unless they were being held against their will.'

He frowned and nodded. 'You never know … '

A long, contemplative silence ensued.

Wendy ruffled the dog behind the ears. 'Has any of this helped you make up your mind?'

He shrugged. 'I still want to dig deeper despite the dangers, but I'm inclined to think the trail went cold on that October night in 1975.'

'How so?'

'Elvis left the building, Wendy.'

She sighed. 'I can see what you're saying, but the mysterious helicopter and the accident with the Land Rover both happened a long time after that. If they *are* accounts of actual events, the Thirlmere base is still in business and up to God knows what.'

'Hmm … you could be onto something there.'

'The King might be in his limo, but the fat lady is still warming up.'

'You've outdone me on the idioms.'

A mischievous smile played across her lips. 'Here's some more: we've talked the talk; how about we walk the walk?'

'Sorry?'

'I was thinking about a return to Thirlmere.'

'Together?'

'Two pairs of eyes are better than one, and I fancy a last crack at Raven Crag.'

He frowned. 'I must admit the helicopter story did get under my skin.'

'I doubt we'll find anything, to be honest, but it's worth a last roll of the dice.'

What harm can it do?

'Okay,' he said. 'When do you want to go?'

'Tomorrow?'

She's keen!

'Tomorrow it is.'

'I'll phone the kennels when we've had some lunch.'

Toby whimpered and pawed her arm.

Colin smiled. 'I think he heard you.'

Chapter Thirty-three

Colin got to the George and Dragon fifteen minutes early and ordered a pint of local real ale. He'd tried to convince himself this wasn't a date, but here he was: in a shirt and sports jacket he'd bought that afternoon and Dutch courage on the bar.

He took a mouthful and made a beeline for a small table.

The alcohol calmed his nerves, but it was found wanting when Wendy arrived.

Jesus H!

She looked great.

A red maxi dress hugged an hour glass figure hitherto concealed by baggy clothing. Chic makeup and the cascade of hair around her shoulders completed a look which turned several heads.

Colin stood up and waved.

She smiled warmly and walked over.

'What can I get you?' he said.

'Vodka and coke, please, lots of ice.'

'Coming up.'

'You've scrubbed up well,' she said.

He blushed. 'You don't look so bad yourself.'

At the bar, he ordered Wendy's drink and another pint.

They dined in an excellent sea food restaurant, where their equally eclectic tastes in music and film made Colin forget his earlier unease. By the time they left, he was about as relaxed as he got these days. His eager intake of strong beer, chardonnay and brandy had hangover written all over it, but he didn't care. Despite their earlier agreement, she'd insisted on splitting the bill. Now he was in a quandary about the significance. Was she just paying her way, or firing a warning shot at a married man with beer goggles? Or was he reading too much into it?

Probably the latter.

When they reached the taxi rank, she turned towards him.

'Thanks for a lovely evening, Colin.'

He raised his hand to his mouth to stifle a burp. 'The pleasure was all mine, Madam.' He opened the taxi door. 'Your carriage awaits.'

She smiled and pecked him on the cheek. 'See you tomorrow.'

He saluted and flashed a lopsided grin. 'Nine o'clock on the dot.'

They waved as the taxi pulled off.

When it turned the corner, he glanced around and realised he'd lost his bearings.

Shit!

Chapter Thirty-four

When they joined the M5, Colin turned down the radio volume. 'If I could avoid this, I would, but we're going to have to call at my house.'

Wendy groaned. 'Why do I not like the sound of that?'

'Sorry, but I need clean clothes and more outdoor gear.'

'It's not going to look good if your wife or daughter clock me.'

'They shouldn't be home when we get there, but I'll phone ahead when we're a bit nearer. If there's a problem, I'll drop you off in town and pick you up when I'm done.'

'Drop me off anyway,' she said. 'Best to play safe.'

They continued in silence for a while.

Then Colin remembered what he'd meant to ask her the day before.

'Can I ask you something?'

'Depends what it is.'

'The framed posters in your lounge.'

'What about them?'

'You tell me.'

She smiled. 'It's not something I bring up in polite company.'

'But you're with *me*.'

She laughed, but a few moments went by before she spoke.

'I believe I have some psychic ability.'

Colin struggled for a suitable response.

'That's the reaction I usually get,' she said dryly.

'I can well imagine.'

'I take it you're a sceptic?'

'I was until Eric Manning possessed one of my employees.'

Wendy shuffled in her seat. 'The thing is: I see people. Most of the time, I don't know if they're dead or alive, but they shouldn't be there regardless. It's difficult to describe because I don't actually see them in the normal way; they're more of a mental imprint.'

'Can you communicate with them?'

'No, but sometimes I feel they want to talk to me.'

'How often does this happen?'

'Half a dozen times a year. That said, the last one was very recent: when we were talking at the harbour, there was a man stood behind you.'

Colin felt a cold chill race up his spine. 'What did he look like?'

'He was your build and around the same age, but he had longer hair and really dark eyes. I think he was wearing a light-coloured shirt with some sort of pattern on it, but I don't get a clear impression of their clothing.'

He ransacked his memory for a match.

'Any ideas?' she said.

'No, but, if you see him again, let me know.'

'Don't worry, I will.'

'How long have you been able to do this?'

'As long I can remember.'

When the conversation resumed, it concerned more trivial matters and gradually petered out until, twenty minutes later, Wendy fell asleep and left Colin alone with his thoughts.

He returned to the description of the man she'd seen at the harbour. One or two possible matches eventually came to mind, but they were alive and well. And why they would want to tail him in some sort of spirit form made no sense whatsoever.

They grabbed lunch at Sandbach services, and then continued on to Cranshaw. Colin didn't hang around in the empty house. He left a gift-wrapped *One Direction* t-shirt on Holly's bed and a brief note for Jan to say he'd taken some clothes and would be in touch soon.

It was a little after five when they arrived at the King's Head.

The brooding, lower slopes of Helvellyn framed a long frontage of whitewashed stucco and lattice windows, nestling under a shallow slate roof.

'Nice to be back?' he said.

She smiled. 'Yeah, it is.'

When he opened the boot, his gaze travelled over the rolling fields and trees across the road, to the distant hills thrown into silhouette by the low sun. He shielded his eyes and scanned each one until he found the bleak outline of Raven Crag.

They dined in the hotel, and then went to Colin's room to study the OS maps. It took less than half an hour to devise a broad search area centred on the crag summit and identify the most likely location for the Land Rover accident.

After a couple of drinks in the bar, Wendy stifled a yawn and said goodnight. There was no kiss this time, but he hadn't expected one. Her attitude had changed since they'd left Cranshaw: a little cooler and less tactile. The detour had underlined his emotional baggage, and its effect on her was understandable.

He went to the bar and ordered another pint.

Chapter Thirty-five

Sunday, 6th April

Colin stopped when they were halfway across the dam and surveyed the reservoir.

Iron-grey fells and dark, wooded slopes girded an expanse of still water daubed with the hazy reflections of sun blushed clouds. Spectral wisps of mist caressed the shoreline, and only the gentle lap of waves disturbed the fragile silence.

He breathed in the cool air. 'You know, I've always thought of Thirlmere as the forgotten mere. When you consider how many people visit the Lake District, it's never that busy here, even in the summer – it's that place you drive past on the way to somewhere else.'

Wendy smiled. 'Wouldn't have it any other way.'

'Neither would I, but I'm starting to wonder if it's had a helping hand.'

'Hmm … I know what you mean.'

'You know how hard it is to find footpaths in these hills.' He pointed high over to the right. 'Even the routes from Derwent Water don't go beyond High Seat or Bleaberry Fell.'

'Tell me about it.'

'Anywhere more remote would have problems with access and infrastructure, but this place ticks all the boxes, not least that nobody in their right mind would suspect what we do.'

'What does that say about us?'

He laughed. 'Guilty as charged.'

The steep forest path skirted the giant slab of scarred rock. At the summit, they took in the impressive view, and then sat down to study their maps. They split the search area into two roughly equal areas, north and south. Wendy volunteered to go north and extend her previous ventures, and Colin took the south. If there was nothing to report, they would get back together and move west towards the open fells.

They retraced their steps to the forest track and stopped at the wooden gate which led to the Iron Age hill fort at Castle Crag.

Colin took a swig of water and studied his phone. 'What's your signal like now?'

'Not good,' Wendy said. 'One bar at best.'

'If you find anything and can't get hold of me, mark it on the map and move on.'

'Okay – all else fails, I'll see you back here in two hours.'

He turned to go. 'Best of luck.'

'You too.'

Colin followed the track for a quarter of a mile, and then descended through the gloomy conifers in a slow, crisscross pattern. He stopped frequently to check the map and admire the views over the reservoir, but nothing untoward caught his attention, and a rocky outcrop suitable for a helicopter landing remained elusive.

It was a little after ten o'clock when his phone rang.

'Hello, Wendy.'

'Colin?' The voice was crackly. 'Can you hear me?'

'Just about.'

'I might've found the place the helicopter landed.'

'Where exactly are you?'

'Hold on a sec ... '

148

Colin strained to hear the coordinates, and then traced his forefinger down and across the map. 'Okay, I'm on my way.'

The rock ledge jutted from the wooded rise like an overturned steam iron.

Colin climbed on top and paced the fissured surface. 'I know sod all about helicopters, but I reckon a small one could land here.' He jumped down and kicked a tree stump. 'There's a fair few of these too – probably cleared to make space for the rotor.'

'That settles it,' Wendy said.

'Which direction do you think the passengers went?'

She blew out her cheeks. 'Now you're asking.'

'Didn't you say the hikers were about to break cover when it landed?'

'That's what I was told.'

'Okay … so, if they were coming from Derwent and had a clear view of the helicopter, they must've sheltered in those trees over there.' He pointed back the way they'd come. 'So I reckon the passengers would've headed in the opposite direction.'

'Come on, then.' Wendy set off. 'Makes sense to me.'

After around a hundred yards, they came to several large boulders, roughly eight feet high, huddled together in the shadows of the crowding conifers.

'What do you think?' Colin said.

'Looks like a natural feature to me, but you never know.'

They walked around it but saw nothing unusual in the smooth rock.

He sighed. 'I'd be more disappointed if I knew what we were looking for.'

She smiled. 'A steel door with a biohazard sign and "Keep Out" in big red letters.'

He took a few steps back and surveyed the boulders. 'If only ... '

Wendy was right: it was just another natural feature that had been here long before people arrived in these islands and would, no doubt, be here when the last one left.

He turned away to survey the trees and caught something in the corner of his right eye. He turned back to the rock, but it'd gone. When he moved his head again, it returned. It was little more than a dark brown smudge, but it seemed to be fixed on the largest boulder.

He edged sideways, tilting and twisting his head in an effort to move the object from his peripheral vision.

'What are you doing, Colin?'

'Bear with me ... I think I'm onto something.'

He froze when the smudge widened and came into focus.

Jesus H!

'Wendy ... '

'Yeah?'

'Look straight at the largest boulder and tell me what you see?'

'Solid rock – sandstone, I think ... '

'Nothing else?'

She shook her head. 'What should I see?'

'One of the symbols from the crashed UFO.'

'You need to see this,' Colin said. 'It's the big triangle with the three circles.'

She strode towards him.

'Stand in front of me,' he said. 'Turn your head to the left slowly but keep looking at the boulder.'

'I'm not getting anything.'

'You'll see it form at the edge of your vision first.'

'Oh, yeah … '

'Now tilt your head back, nice and slow.'

'It's getting clearer … there's definitely something … Holy shit!

'So I'm not imagining things.'

'Definitely not. It's just like Seth Hartford described … '

She turned away and pulled a crumpled handkerchief from her pocket.

He waited until she'd dried her eyes, and then put his arm around her shoulder. 'Your dad was spot on, wasn't he?'

She managed a fragile smile. 'You know, I never doubted it, but this final proof makes me realise just how much I miss him.'

He pulled her to him gently, and they hugged with her warm cheek against his.

Colin could've held her for longer, a lot longer, but they parted without any awkwardness and walked back to the boulder.

She ran her fingers across the stone. 'When Eric first visited the sphere, didn't one of the symbols morph into a doorway?'

'It did,' he said. 'Which means the alien technology has been adapted for human use.'

'But we can only see it from ten feet away at the edge of our vision.'

'Not exactly user friendly, is it?'

'The people in the helicopter must've used it.'

'No doubt,' he said. 'The question is: how?'

'Christ only knows.' She took off her rucksack and sat down. 'Let's chill for a bit and talk it through.'

'Good idea.'

He took off his and reached inside for an energy bar. He grinned when his hand brushed against the plastic bag.

I wonder ...

He pulled it out and eased the helmet free.

She lowered her water bottle. 'Is that what I think it is?'

He nodded. 'The one Josh found in the shop.'

'Why did you bring it *here*?'

'I haven't let it out of my sight since Ron died.'

'Have you tried it?'

'Not yet, but now's as good a time as any.'

Wendy reached up and took it from him. 'It's a bit Heath Robinson, isn't it?'

'Just a bit, but he got it to work.'

'What's inside the little disks?'

'I assume solenoids because they magnetise when you switch it on. I think the circuit board splits the voltage between them to create an alternating magnetic field. There's not a lot of power involved, so the wave pattern is probably the critical feature.'

'There's more at the back than the front.'

'That might be down to the fact that images are processed in the back of the brain.'

'Where did a toy shop owner learn how to make this?'

'Ron Vine said he did a lot of research.'

'So he mastered neurology and electronics?'

'I wouldn't say *mastered*, but he learned enough to do what he wanted to, no doubt with a great deal of trial and error.'

She shrugged. 'I wouldn't rule out somebody else being involved.'

'Ron never said anything.'

'He mightn't have known.'

'True, but if Eric did refer to experts or academics, it's likely he kept them in the dark about its true purpose.'

She passed the helmet back to him. 'Maybe.'

He placed it on his head. 'Probably best if you switch it on for me. And keep your finger primed; you might have to turn it off quickly if I scream or faint.'

She got to her feet. 'Understood.'

He turned his back to her. 'Flick the switch, Igor.'

'Yes, Master, but less of the "Igor" and more of "my glamorous assistant", if you don't mind.'

'Duly noted.'

He heard the click and took a deep breath.

'Anything?'

'My scalp's tingling a bit, but, apart from that … hold on, something's happening … '

He steadied himself against the rock and stared into the distance.

She put her hand on his back. 'Are you okay?'

'Bit dizzy and I've got this weird tunnel vision.'

'Do you want me to switch it off?'

'No, not yet.' He took a deep breath, and then stood up straight and turned towards the boulder. 'Wow – I

153

can see it – it's a deep gold colour and the outline's razor sharp – it seems to be floating just off the surface, but – '

'Is it doing anything?'

'It's not morphing into a door, if that's what you mean.' Colin reached out his hand. 'Maybe if I touch it ... '

His fingers passed through the symbol without effect.

'Okay ... let's try this ... '

He traced the outline of the triangle with his forefinger.

'Oh, my God,' she said. '*I* can see it now.'

The symbol grew and merged into a sharp rectangle about six feet tall by three wide.

Then it sank into the rock, leaving a smooth sided passageway in its wake.

Chapter Thirty-seven

An eerie silence seemed to envelope the boulders.

Colin reached around and switched the helmet off at the third attempt. He removed it slowly and ran his fingers through his hair without taking his eyes off the passageway.

What the fuck have I just done?

'Should I go first?' Wendy said.

He swallowed hard. 'My bottle's gone.'

She squeezed his arm. 'I'm bricking it too, but this is what we came for.'

'Is it?'

'What do you mean?'

'I thought we might find an intriguing feature up here, something to discuss back at the pub. But this? What kind of Pandora's Box have we, quite literally, opened?'

'I've come too far to walk away, Colin.'

'If we go in there, we'll lose that option.'

'I *have* to do this,' she said. 'With or without you.'

Crystal clear images of Holly and Jan flashed into his mind.

'I know, I know …'

In a desperate play for time, he slipped the helmet into the plastic bag and returned it to his rucksack. *Come on! Get your act together!*

She walked into the passageway.

That settles it …

He took a last look at the sun dappled conifers and followed her.

The daylight only penetrated a few yards into the inky darkness.

She stopped and turned around. 'We're going to need the torches.'

Before he could reply, the entrance closed and everything went black.

He clenched his teeth and fought the rising panic.

A moment later, the walls and ceiling began to glow pale blue.

Behind a tree, around thirty yards from the outcrop, a man lowered his binoculars and pulled a small walkie-talkie from his waterproof jacket.

'Raven Four to Command.'

There was a brief crackle before the reply: 'Come in, Raven Four. Over.'

'Report: two persons have accessed Gateway Alpha. Over.'

'Say again, Raven Four. Over.'

'Two persons have accessed Gateway Alpha. Over.'

'Roger, Raven Four. Describe. Over.'

'Adult male, adult female, dressed for hiking. Over.'

'Remain in position, Raven Four. Over.'

'Wilco. Out.'

He raised his binoculars and scanned the outcrop.

Colin's fear subsided when he ran his fingers along the wall. 'I've never seen anything like this. It's as if the rock itself is emitting light.'

Wendy touched it. 'It's quite warm, isn't it?'

'And glassy smooth, which makes me wonder if it *is* rock.'

'Whatever it is, somebody knows we're here.'

'Maybe,' he said. 'But it might be an automated system.'

'Come on, let's find out.'

They walked in silence.

After around fifty yards, the blue glow ended abruptly. Beyond was pitch black.

They stopped to remove each other's torches from the rucksacks and stepped into a rough-hewn cavern around thirty feet in diameter and twenty in height. Most of the interior, from floor to roof, was taken up by a rusty structure made from three square sections stacked one on top of the other and held together by huge bolts. Several thick pipes curved down from flanges in the roof into the top section. The bottom section housed a brushed steel door with a small keypad at the side. An oily, metallic odour filled the air.

'I don't get it,' he said. 'We've just interacted with alien technology, and now we're in something that looks like a forty-year-old power station.'

'You read my thoughts.'

He stabbed the lifeless keys. 'And something tells me it hasn't been used for quite some time.'

She shone her torch at the door. 'This door hasn't fully closed.'

They eased their fingers into the gap and heaved it open.

Six thick steel cables plunged into a shaft deeper than their torches could reach.

He sighed. 'Doesn't look good, does it?'

'There must be another way,' she said.

They split up and walked around the cavern in opposite directions. At the back, they met at a metal door with a long handle. It opened onto an unlit concrete stairwell, which wound down through the rock in a succession of narrow landings. They descended two levels and found another door. He opened it and shone his torch down a long corridor with at least half a dozen open doors on each side. The tiled floor was strewn with manila folders and sheets of paper.

Colin went through and picked up a document stamped *Classified* in red.

He held the torch to his shoulder and scanned it.

Wendy joined him. 'What's it say?'

'Don't know,' he said. 'I can't read Russian.'

Chapter Thirty-eight

London SW1

Section Controller 08A Anderson rapped the table with an impatient staccato and scanned his four colleagues hunched over their inch-thick reports. The flutter of turning pages played against a backdrop of dyspeptic rumbles from the ancient air-conditioning system which strived to ensure the temperature in his subterranean office was never quite right.

'Oh dear, oh dear,' he said. 'I was under the assumption you would have actually *read* the documentation before dragging yourselves here today.'

A heavy woman, with short, blonde hair, looked up. 'Sorry, Eight, but we didn't get them until late yesterday.'

Anderson tutted and glanced at his watch. 'As you all know, everything must be shredded before you leave, so I wouldn't bank on keeping any luncheon appointments.'

A murmur of resigned consent rumbled around the table.

The page fluttering continued.

At the far end, a gaunt young man cleared his throat. 'Page ninety-eight – paragraph four, sub section three.'

'Speak.'

'I was under the impression MI5 had taken this under their wing.'

Anderson sighed. 'Alas, no. I'm afraid we still have that dubious honour despite my earnest protestations.'

'But I received an email on Friday which – '

A sharp knock at the door stymied his announcement.

A smartly-dressed, middle-aged woman entered. 'Sorry to interrupt, sir, but I've just received a message that can't wait.'

Anderson flashed a perfunctory smile. 'What does it concern?'

His secretary glanced around the room with a troubled expression.

'You may speak freely here,' he said.

She frowned. 'It's a code one.'

The fluttering stopped.

Anderson got to his feet and followed her out of the room.

Five hundred miles away, Professor Alex Jeprell stepped through the heavy wooden door and lit a cigarette in the shelter of the stone arch. He took a long, contemplative drag, and then strolled along the flagged path to the cliff edge and sat down on the solitary wooden bench. He'd allowed himself five cigarettes a day for longer than he cared to remember, but, over the last six months, it had crept up to twelve; and considerably more when he drank wine, which was another burgeoning indulgence. He came here when he needed to think, and he'd done a lot of that lately. Time was ebbing like the tide, and funds had dwindled with little hope of replenishment. So much promise had turned to set back after set back, and morale was at an all-time low. Even he was losing hope.

He gazed out to sea and wondered, as he'd done so many times, what lay beneath: what scuttled and swam over folded sand, and seethed and plotted between cold rock and swaying weed. Sometimes, he felt them in his mind, coaxing and probing his innermost thoughts. Even in such isolation, the local rumours had reached him, and they weren't the imaginings of excited children or the mistaken sightings of weary, rain-lashed fishermen. They were real. And they weren't going away. The question was: why?

His phone rang.

He dragged it from the pocket of his lab coat and flicked the cigarette away.

The number wasn't the one he'd expected.

'Jeprell.'

'Professor Jeprell, we have a priority comms intercept that requires your urgent attention.'

'Where and what did you intercept?'

'Thirlmere, code one.'

He felt his chest tighten. 'Speak.'

Chapter Thirty-nine

Colin passed the document to Wendy.

'It's heavily redacted,' she said. 'But you're not wrong.'

'Is it dated?'

'Err, yeah … can't read the month, but the year's 1983.'

'Could the old Soviet Union have been mixed up in this?'

'Christ knows.' She picked up another. 'This one's in English – but it's just a memo about the service schedule for the heating system.'

They strolled along the corridor, raking the floor and offices with their torches. They picked up documents and folders here and there, but all of them were either censored or concerned with mundane clerical matters and dropped after cursory glances. The small offices were basically furnished and meant for single occupants.

At the end, they entered a much larger one filled with neat rows of computer workstations and filing cabinets. More discarded paperwork littered the floor.

Wendy opened a filing cabinet and peered inside.

Colin strolled up and down the office. 'These PCs are at least ten years old.'

'Doesn't surprise me,' she said. 'I haven't seen a document dated later than 2003.'

'I had all kinds of ideas about what we'd find in here, but this definitely wasn't it.'

'Same here,' she said. 'I'd psyched myself up for a run-in with security guards and brainiacs in white coats.

I can't quite decide if I should be relieved or disappointed.'

He sat down on a swivel chair and flicked through a tray of CDs in plastic cases and floppy disks. The coded labels offered no clues to their contents.

She shut the filing cabinet and turned towards him. 'We won't find anything here.'

'Agreed,' he said. 'And it looks like we're free to roam at will.'

They left the office and returned to the stairwell.

When the door closed behind them, Colin froze.

'Kill your torch,' he whispered.

'Why?' she mimed.

'Just bear with me.'

They switched off their torches.

'It's not completely dark, is it?' she said softly.

He leaned over the hand rail. 'There's a light two floors down.'

They made a cautious descent to a landing lit by a small red lamp above another door.

Colin gripped the handle and opened it slowly.

More wall-mounted, red lamps illuminated another deserted corridor.

He turned to Wendy. 'Must be the emergency lights.'

They went through and switched on their torches.

The floor was free from discarded documents, and the offices on either side looked as nondescript as the ones upstairs.

Halfway along, he stopped and sighed. 'Doesn't look hopeful, does it?'

She took a few more steps. 'Don't know though … '

'Sorry?'

'What do you think *that* is?'

He followed her torch beam to a dark, arcing splash along the left wall.

'Hard to say,' he said. 'There's some on the floor too.'

'And more over here,' she said.

Her torch had found a larger smeared stain. Just above its highest reach, something glinted in the disk of light.

Colin probed the hole with his forefinger, and a cold, hard object met his touch. He scraped away the surrounding plaster and pulled out the flattened bullet.

'Is that what I think it is?' she said.

He nodded and tossed it away.

'I just knew it was blood,' she said.

'It *had* crossed my mind.'

They raked their torches around the walls and doors and found five more bullet holes.

Wendy shook her head. 'What the hell happened here?'

'Christ only knows,' he said. 'But somebody moved the bodies.'

'And abandoned the base?'

'Certainly looks that way.'

She wrinkled her nose and turned to the nearest door. 'Can you smell that?'

He sniffed the air and frowned. 'What're you getting?'

'Ripe kitchen bin.' She strode into the office. 'Colin, get your arse in here.'

He followed her into an office dominated by a long table enclosed by plastic chairs. At the far end, under a sagging projector screen, empty food cans, discarded clothing and paperback books surrounded a crumpled sleeping bag.

'Looks like we're not on our – '

A sudden commotion spun them around.

A dark figure dashed from the room.

'What the – ?' Colin blurted and went after it.

'Hey!' Wendy yelled. 'Come back!'

In the corridor, Colin came to his senses and pulled up.

He grabbed Wendy's arm as she went past. 'Let him go!' She struggled, but he tugged her back. 'He could be dangerous!'

The figure stopped at the stairwell door and reached for the handle but didn't turn it.

Nobody moved or spoke for what seemed like an age.

Colin took a few measured steps.

'We're not looking for you,' he said. 'We just want to talk … '

The man turned around slowly.

Chapter Forty

He was taller and stockier than Colin, but looked about thirty years older. A scruffy white beard framed a pale, wrinkled face. Rheumy eyes flickered under the long peak of a frayed baseball cap. His jeans and parka were filthy, and the pungent odour of a long unwashed body carried on the stale air.

'Who are you?' Wendy said. 'What're you doing here?'

'I could ask you the same questions,' he said.

His accent was hard to place, but Colin thought he'd heard a hint of Welsh.

Another awkward silence.

'Who're you with?' the man said.

'With?' Colin said. 'We're not with anybody.'

'I find that hard to believe.'

'We're not involved in any of this,' Wendy said.

'Then how did you get in here?'

'How did *you*?'

'I used to work here,' the man said. 'I got left behind when it was decommissioned.'

'Left behind?' Colin said.

'It's a long story. How you got in here is a far more urgent matter with potentially very serious consequences.'

'We opened a passageway,' she said. 'On a rock three to four hundred yards north of Castle Crag.'

The man narrowed his eyes. 'How exactly?'

Colin eased the rucksack from his back and removed the plastic bag. He pulled the helmet free and offered it to him.

He took it and held it up to one of the red lamps.

Colin noticed his hands were trembling. 'It might look a bit rough and ready, but, when I put it on, I could see the alien symbol. I traced the big triangle with my finger, and it transformed into the passageway.'

The man studied the battery and circuit board. 'Was there anybody else out there?'

'Not that we know of,' Colin said.

'No other hikers?'

'Haven't seen a soul since we left the reservoir.'

'Tell me more about this.'

'I'll do my best,' Colin said. 'But I know next to nothing about how it works. The bloke who made it has been dead for forty years. He used it for some form of mental time travel, but entities with the same technology as the ones brought here intercepted one of his trips and befriended him, but when they – '

'If he's been dead that long, how do you know this?'

'I doubt you'd believe me if I told you.'

The man frowned and lowered the helmet. 'What did these entities look like?'

'Apparently, they appeared as luminous blue humanoids in a circular room lined with the same symbols Seth Hartford saw.'

'Who?'

'The bloke who found the crash site in the Cascades.'

The man flashed a wry smile. 'Bill Klein's pet project.'

'That's him.'

'So how did you find this place?'

'That's down to me,' Wendy said. 'My father worked on the Oregon craft – he was the one that blew the whistle to Klein.'

The man looked shocked, but his expression quickly changed to one of concern. 'Are you his *only* child?'

'Yeah. Why do you ask?'

He frowned. 'It's not important.'

Colin suspected the opposite but decided not to challenge him just yet.

'What do you know about my father?'

'Not much, I'm afraid. Even his name was classified. I started here a few months after he left, but I heard what happened through the grapevine.'

'Was he despised for what he did?'

'Officially, he was persona non grata, but, in private, there was some genuine sympathy for what he tried to do.'

Wendy managed a fragile smile. 'Thanks – that's good to know.'

The man scratched his beard. 'So how did you two get together?'

'I tracked her down,' Colin said. 'When I made the connection with the symbols.'

'You've done well to get this far, but what lies within will hasten you across the Rubicon – it's not too late to turn back.'

A wave of doubt washed through Colin.

'It's personal with me,' Wendy said. 'I'm strapped in tight.'

'I thought as much.' He turned to Colin. 'You don't look so sure.'

Colin glanced at Wendy and smiled. 'What she said.'

The man handed the helmet back. 'Let's take a seat.'

They returned to the office, where he gestured at the long table. 'I don't want to know your names, and I won't be divulging mine. The reason should become clear soon enough.'

Colin and Wendy sat down next to each other. They switched off their torches when he brought a wind up lantern from the back of the room and took a seat opposite.

She spoke first. 'Is there anybody else in here?'

The man shook his head. 'This is the first conversation I've had in eight years.'

'What in God's name happened?'

The man sighed. 'It wasn't in God's name, I can assure you of that, but people tried to play God nevertheless. Terrible things happen when disparate civilisations are thrust into contact.' He turned to Wendy. 'I assume your father said as much.'

'We never discussed it,' she said. 'I only found out about his involvement after he died a couple of years ago.'

The man's concerned expression returned. 'I imagine there's a lot you want to ask.'

She blew out her cheeks. 'Where do I start?'

Colin shuffled in his seat. 'How about the blood and bullet holes?'

'Things got out of hand when the base was closed.'

'Go on.'

'Trust me; we need to build up to that.'

'Okay,' Colin said. 'Let's start at the very beginning. Why did they crash? One is bad enough, but another twelve years later beggars belief.'

'You don't know about the third one?'

Colin glanced at Wendy, but her narrowed eyes remain fixed on the man.

'There were *three*?' he said.

The man nodded. 'They arrived at twelve year intervals, hitting the ground in a wide arc over the northern hemisphere: the first in Oregon, the second Scotland and the third Siberia in the spring of 1975. The crew from the Oregon crash told us to expect the others, but it was only known to a select few. Apparently, they jumped to and from dimensions to travel interstellar distances, but these three got caught in a temporal wave; a localised ripple in space-time that hit them in a succession of peaks and troughs they couldn't evade. It threw them out over the earth about five thousand miles apart but chronologically skewed in line with its wavelength.'

'I take it this wasn't a *completely* random event?'

'What do you mean?'

'It just dumped them on a populated planet?'

'Apparently, they were headed here. The temporal wave disrupted their drive systems, which made the spheres difficult to control. They managed to steer clear of any populated areas and hit the ground not too far from where they'd intended to land. We weren't sure if the other two would drop onto a city or end up at the bottom of the sea. Thankfully, they avoided either scenario, and we got to them before anybody else.'

'Where did they come from?'

'NGC 6791: an open star cluster in the Lyra constellation some 13,000 light years from here. For concision, we referred to them as Lyrans.'

'Why did they come here?'

'Passive observation, allegedly. They hadn't planned any direct contact, but the crash landings put paid to that. Their drive systems self-repaired, but they wouldn't leave until the third craft arrived. In the meantime, we had access to alien know-how. Or so we thought. Unfortunately, their technology was so far removed from ours that it was nigh on impossible to glean anything of practical import. Initially, we assumed they'd simply progressed further along a path of scientific discovery that the human race was due to tread. But we were so wrong. They'd chosen a radically different route around the time they mastered nuclear fusion, and it soon became clear that evolved savannah apes aren't intellectually equipped to understand the universe the way they did. They'd achieved this insight by bypassing evolution and redesigning their biology from the ground up – their brains were cybernetic; part organic and part electronics, but the integration was on the molecular level.'

Wendy leaned forward. 'My father said they could morph into any shape.'

'A slight exaggeration, but they could take whatever form was appropriate for their requirements. The only restriction was their large brains which remained the same regardless of morphology. Their home planet was similar to ours, but invertebrate life got a foothold there before anything else. They'd evolved from a group of animals similar to cephalopods.'

'Octopus and squid?'

'That's right, but they left the sea and developed lungs and a tough outer skin. It was the most popular form they took for locomotion and basic manipulation; a sort of race memory that had resisted the genetic engineering. They could adapt to just about any environment and were sustained by a concentrated mix of hydrocarbons and metallic compounds which they stored close to their brains. The by-products were partly recycled, but their metabolism was an order of magnitude more efficient than ours, and the depletion

171

rate was extremely slow. They could self-repair all but the gravest cerebral damage and were, by all practical measures, immortal. Reproduction was rarely instigated and non-sexual; they effectively cloned themselves.'

'It seems to me you learned more about their biology than their technology.'

'We did, and there lies the root of the problem that trapped me here.'

After a few moments, the man continued: 'In the late sixties, the UK and US bases pooled their resources into a project called H3S. The aim was to enhance the human brain to a point where we could tap into their knowledge, but the Lyrans refused to get involved and seemed content to count the days until they could leave. We were faced with the biggest anti-climax in history: the first contact with advanced extra-terrestrials, and we learn next to nothing. We were just a holding pen; somewhere for them to wait for their buddies to arrive, and then skedaddle. Human civilisation was of little, if any, interest to them. We, on the other hand, were desperate to know what – '

'Who are *we* exactly?' Wendy said. 'Who's behind all this?'

'Now there's a question,' the man said. 'And not one I can answer in detail. You see, most of what I know is pretty toxic, and, believe it or not, there are gaps I've had to fill with educated guesses.'

'How is it toxic?' Colin said.

'It's best you don't know. Trust me, ignorance can be bliss.'

'Try us,' Wendy said.

The man frowned and nodded. 'The organisation I worked for doesn't even have an official name; it was always referred to as *The Group* – let's just say it's an apolitical, trans-national cabal that operates under intense secrecy. It was formed at the end of World War Two to investigate the Foo Fighter phenomenon. At first, it was an Anglo-American affair, but the Soviets were brought in after the Scottish crash – less than a year after Cuba, but this trumped even a nuclear face off.'

'How were *you* recruited?' Colin said.

'Oh, the usual, humdrum way: groomed by a tutor at Cambridge. Over thirty years I gave them to end up like a rat in a cage, scared of my own shadow.'

'How did it get to that?'

'Bear with me,' he said. 'Shortly after the Siberian crash, the Lyrans announced their departure and requested the spheres be moved from the bases, so they could leave the earth's atmosphere and make the dimensional jump. The Group's controllers refused to comply until they helped with H3S, and a standoff ensued. It also opened up a rift at grassroots level. I was with the faction in favour of letting them go, but our opposition fell on deaf ears. The Lyrans were benign, but they warned all three bases they would employ alternative methods to leave that could be highly destructive. They returned to their spheres, and the standoff continued until the autumn of 1975. On the night of October the twenty-second, localised spatial distortions were observed close to the spheres in all three bases – '

Colin's heart missed a beat.

' – They grew steadily into large black ellipses that swallowed each one, and then closed. Well that's what happened in the US and Soviet bases. Here, something went badly wrong. When the ellipse started to close, there was an intense burst of energy that fried just about every electrical circuit in the base. Even the back-up generators and emergency lights failed. At least a dozen people were badly injured, and, although the craft appeared undamaged, its crew were toast. We never found out what happened and could only theorise how the others had made their escape.'

Colin glanced at Wendy.

She gestured towards the man. 'Tell him.'

He cleared his throat. 'I might be able to shed some light on it.'

'I'm listening,' the man said.

'The bloke who made the helmet was instructed by the blue entities to build a machine. I was told by his friend, who actually witnessed its operation, that it caused an elliptical distortion in space, and something spoke to him from inside it. His friend destroyed the machine; however, we believe the engineering company which made the components built another one that melted the prototype shop the night you had the energy burst here. In the early hours of the following morning, two bright orbs were seen over the town. Apparently, they even showed up on the radar at Manchester Airport.'

'Where did this occur?'

'Cranshaw, about eighty miles south of here.'

The man scratched his beard. 'Did he describe the machine?'

Colin pulled a plastic wallet from his rucksack and gave it to him.

He removed the printouts and studied them. 'Incredible … absolutely incredible … we never guessed they were up to something like this. You see, those creatures possessed a consciousness that transcended our three dimensional perception. If they sensed another entity had entered their space, so to speak, it might well have instigated the escape plan.'

Colin rolled his eyes. 'So Eric might've unwittingly given them the idea.'

'Eric?'

'The bloke who made the helmet.'

'Most likely,' the man said. 'What salts the wound is that we built several not dissimilar mechanisms during the 1980s without success.'

'I thought you learned next to nothing about their technology.'

'We knew the symbols had trans-dimensional properties and electromagnetism was the key to their activation, but we were clutching at straws.'

'What about the passageway?' Wendy said. 'That's clearly alien technology.'

The man eased a small torch from his parka. 'I think it's time for the guided tour.'

The man led them back to the stairwell, where they descended another two floors to a set of sturdy double doors. He pushed through and beckoned them into a short, narrow corridor lit by more red lamps. At the end, a blush of weak light picked out a thin metal handrail which seemed to be floating in absolute darkness. The air was noticeably cooler, and Colin could hear liquid dripping onto a hard surface.

The man reached for something out of sight.

A band of powerful lights burst into life around a huge cylindrical cavity at least forty yards across and fifty feet deep.

He stepped onto a strip of dimpled steel plate and gripped the handrail. 'Welcome to Area 62.'

Colin and Wendy exchanged expectant glances and joined him.

The walkway encircled the cavity and connected to another one about ten feet below via four equispaced staircases. More staircases led down from the lower walkway to the floor. Shuttered windows and solid metal doors lined the two upper levels. Columns of galvanised ducting and rusty pipework reached up to what appeared to be four air conditioning units bolted to a framework of girders above their heads.

'Area 62?' Wendy said. 'I take it there's a connection with Area 51?'

The man nodded. 'The official name is EICUK6201, but Area 62 was pithier, and even the controllers started to use it after a while – a smidgeon of humour in a place otherwise devoid of it – *62* refers to the year the base was officially reopened, but it dates back to World

War One. This chamber was originally used to test poison gases. After the war, it was mothballed until the mid-1930s, and then operated again until 1949 when a more advanced facility was built in Yorkshire. When the Americans told us to expect the crash in Scotland, this place was deemed to be the best option, but it took eight years to prepare and was only just ready when the sphere hit the highlands. It was brought here at night, by a twin-engine Chinook, to a purpose made entrance up at Sippling Crag.'

'How many people worked here?' Wendy asked.

'It varied quite a bit, but no more than a hundred at most.'

'That doesn't sound a lot.'

'The Group was, by necessity, small and very select. Expenditure was never a problem, and decisions were made quickly – a little too quickly sometimes.'

Colin leaned over the handrail. The bottom level was featureless except for a set of heavy duty, rust-streaked doors easily wide enough for three cars.

'What's behind the big doors?'

The man winked. 'All in good time.'

They followed him to the nearest staircase and descended to the next level. He opened one of the solid doors and walked into a vestibule. He went through another door on the right and held it open for them. Colin noticed another lifeless keypad at the side.

Recessed ceiling lights flickered and revealed a room about forty feet square and very different from the ones they'd seen so far.

Two wide laboratory benches, lined with dusty glass vessels of various shapes and sizes, ran the full length of the room. The largest vessels were around four feet tall and half that in diameter. Each one rested in a metal frame and was fed by an array of plastic hoses; whatever they'd been connected to had evidently been removed, leaving them strewn across the bench tops like multi-coloured spaghetti. Severed copper pipes and power cables jutted and drooped from the cracked white walls. Breathing masks and rubber gloves spilled from crumpled cartons on the vinyl floor.

The man kicked one of the cartons. 'This is just one of the base's five laboratories. The expensive equipment was removed when it closed.'

'What were the glass jars for?' Wendy said.

'Incubation.'

'Of what?'

'What indeed.' He surveyed the laboratory with a forlorn expression. 'The events of 1975 presented an unexpected opportunity, namely five dead extraterrestrials to study in the utmost secrecy, free from any ethical, moral or legal restraints. What's not to like?'

Colin peered into one of the largest vessels. 'How long have you got?'

'That was my position, and I wasn't alone. But The Group ploughed on regardless. The Lyrans were built from sixteen autosomal chromosome pairs. That's six less than us, and we have an extra sexual pair. But theirs were significantly more complex and seemingly exempt from the types of mutation that drive natural selection. Attempts to clone them were ill-conceived and unsuccessful, so the attention turned to human-alien hybrids, and, once again, we split into two factions. I was with the one that wanted more discussion and restraints, but several high-ranking Americans relocated here, and they were right behind the project. I'm not a religious man, but I *am* an ethical one, and it was

179

difficult to stomach the Frankenstein-like debacles I had to witness.' He surveyed the vessels. 'Some of their creations died in agony in this very room.'

'What was *your* role in all this?' Wendy said.

'My background is unusual in that I have doctorates in both electronic engineering and human biology. I headed up a small team charged with investigating how their brain cells interacted with a byzantine matrix of nanoconductors.'

'And how far did you get?'

'Not that far, if I'm honest, and it took the best part of twenty years, but we learned enough to provide some critical data to The Group.'

'To what effect?'

'A batch of successful hybrids and the closure of this base.'

Colin frowned. 'They shut it down after a major breakthrough?'

The man nodded. 'Its location had been in question since the early-nineties. In 1963, the amount of tourism in this area was a fraction of what it was thirty years later, and the movement of supplies and personnel became a logistical nightmare. We were earmarked for closure by 2010, by which time the various departments would've been split up and incorporated into existing sites, not necessarily in this country. It was widely known that certain people weren't happy with these plans, and the breakthrough with the hybrids brought everything to a head.' He took a deep nasal breath. 'Before we get into all that, allow me to take you quite literally out of this world.'

Chapter Forty-three

They left the laboratory and descended to the bottom of the cavity.

The man strode across the smooth concrete floor and stopped at the steel doors. 'If what you've seen and heard so far hasn't changed your lives forever, this will.'

Wendy nudged Colin. 'What's he getting at?'

'Let's wait and see,' he said.

His heart was beating faster now.

The man tapped a keypad at the side and flattened his palm on a small screen.

The reluctant groan of steel on steel reverberated around the cavity, and the doors began to slide apart. Colin saw a tangram of metal surfaces shimmer under harsh lights.

The gap grew, inch by inch, to reveal a large, faceted sphere.

'Oh my God,' Wendy whispered.

Colin's breath caught in his throat.

The man beckoned them to join him.

They walked through the widening gap into a short passageway which opened onto another cylindrical cavity around sixty feet across and forty high. The sphere was between twenty and thirty feet in diameter and rested on a squat steel frame at the centre of the cavity. A thin ladder, bolted to the frame, reached halfway up. Colin's gaze roamed over a giant ball of flawless polygons and razor sharp edges. There were no other discernible features.

'A perfect truncated icosahedron,' the man said. 'Twenty regular hexagonal faces and twelve regular pentagonal faces, intersecting at ninety seamless edges. The entire thing weighs no more than a small hatchback.'

Wendy walked around it at a respectful distance.

Colin fought to contain a giddy mix of trepidation and unprecedented awe.

He approached it with measured steps and hopped onto the steel frame. He ran his fingers over a pentagonal face which spanned about six feet from corner to corner. The material had the appearance of finely-polished steel but felt warmer and oddly organic. He noticed his hand wasn't reflected in the surface. He moved his head closer, but nothing stared back.

'You see the lack of reflectivity,' the man said.

'Yeah … it's really weird.'

'It reacts to light but doesn't reflect it in the conventional sense.'

Colin scanned the sphere. 'I can't see the symbols.'

'Move your head so that it's parallel to any of the hexagonal faces, then tilt it from side to side very slowly – they'll show up at some point.'

He did as instructed and held his pose when it came into view. He did the same with an adjacent face and saw a different symbol. They were larger than the one on the rock but had the same deep gold colour and seemed to be floating just above the surface.

He turned to the man when Wendy reappeared. 'Can we get inside?'

'Of course.' The man went to the ladder and climbed to the top. 'This technique will be familiar to you.' He reached out his right forefinger and traced a large triangle across a hexagonal face. 'Bear with me; I haven't done this for quite a while.' He leaned back and smiled. 'Well, well – right first time.'

A tiny hole appeared at the centre of the face. It grew into a small hexagon and continued to expand until it reached the edges. There was no hint of anything mechanical; it was as if that particular face had dematerialised.

The man stepped off the ladder and ducked inside. 'Mind the gap.'

Colin and Wendy didn't wait for an invite.

He let her go first and watched with growing anticipation as she entered the sphere.

As he reached the top of the ladder, the first thing that struck him was the thinness of the hull: it could only have been two millimetres at most. The man's warning wasn't tongue in cheek: there was a gap of about a foot between the hull and the internal floor.

His heart was thumping fast when he stepped across.

The interior was constructed from the same metallic material and lit by a soft ambient light with no visible source or cast shadows. The floor resembled a thin wheel with a pentagonal axle at its centre; five wide spokes connected the hub to the rim, and each one supported an identical structure not unlike an open, angular cocoon embedded in a multi-faceted pedestal indented with three holes on each side. At floor level and just above their heads, the axle branched into five horizontal arms which merged with the cocoons and a shallow ring running around the inside of the hull. Through the tapered gaps in the floor, Colin saw that it connected, in the same way, to an identical ring underneath. There were no recognisable controls or instrumentation.

The man went to the axle and held out his arms. 'This entire structure and the hull can spin and rotate independently of each other, not unlike a giant gyroscope. We're actually floating on two powerful, localised fields between the upper and lower rings and the hull's internal surface. The physics of this balanced repulsion was never fully understood. Other than that, not one moving part in the entire bloody thing.' He pointed at one of the cocoons. 'The crew morphed their bodies into these chairs and plugged their tentacles, for want of a better word, into the holes at the sides. How they actually interfaced and operated this thing is a mystery they never divulged and we were unable to ascertain – without them, it's just a big lump of incomprehensible alloy.'

Colin and Wendy walked up and down the spokes, gawping like children in a sweet shop. The interior exuded a palpable atmosphere he couldn't quite put his finger on but called to mind the esoteric serenity of an empty church. The air had an ionised tang to it like the clean taste left by an electrical storm.

'I'm lost for words,' Colin said barely above a whisper. 'But I doubt there are any to describe how I feel right now.'

'I'll second that,' Wendy said in an equally hushed tone.

Nobody spoke for a few moments.

'Why is it still here?' Colin said.

'It has to be somewhere, and this is as good a place as any.'

'Mothballed in an abandoned base?'

The man smiled. 'You mean: instead of surrounded by teams of boffins dedicated to unlocking its secrets in some ultramodern facility.'

'You're on the right lines.'

'We passed that stage a long time ago. Without the crew, it's practically inert and totally unresponsive to any invasive or passive procedures. A colleague once observed that it was like landing a fighter jet in the Amazon rain forest and asking the local tribe to swap the flight control system.'

'But you opened it by tracing out the symbol.'

The man nodded. 'Just like you did with the gateway. Have you asked yourself why you did that?'

Colin shrugged. 'It never crossed my mind.'

'It did,' the man said. 'But you weren't aware of it.'

'Not sure I follow.'

'A great deal of psychological testing was carried out by our Soviet comrades, which identified some unusual sub-conscious brain activity in humans and primates when the symbols were viewed for more than a few seconds. More focussed research and some tortuous mathematics brought us to the conclusion that they're actually fundamental structural features of a universe we only see in part. This meant the Lyrans had discovered rather than invented them and found a way of controlling their properties to manipulate space and time in a variety of ways.'

'So the tracing motion is a sort of reflex?'

'In a way, but it only works on the big triangle with the three linked circles, which, as you now know, can restructure solid objects. The activation is disarmingly simple, almost naive, but the movement of your arm describes a three dimensional interface with the symbol and triggers a short-lived burst of electromagnetism from this craft. This spawned countless theories, none of which stood up to experimental scrutiny. The other four symbols remain a mystery, but they must have their own explicit properties and applications, and we didn't rule out their use in combination like a code or equation. It's all about how multi-dimensional geometries intersect with one other under the influence of magnetic fields, but a brain that only perceives length, breadth and height is hamstrung from the start.'

'So the Lyrans created the gateway?'

The man nodded. 'After the original access points were compromised by a couple of close shaves with hikers. There are two of them: the one you came through and a much larger one to the south for vehicle access. It was only ever used at night, and United Utilities know it's a restricted area and keep well away. It goes without saying that we couldn't see the triangles head on, but, under the Lyran's guidance, we added small indentations in the rock at the three apex points. They're easy to spot if you know what you're looking for, but next to impossible if you don't.'

'We did see the symbol,' Colin said. '*Without* the helmet.'

'From the corner of your eye?'

'That's right,' Wendy said. 'With our heads skewed to one side.'

'I'm impressed. They're harder to see than the ones on the sphere and most find it difficult even under instruction.'

She frowned. 'Why *are* they so elusive?'

'Good question,' the man said. 'The best way to explain it is with an analogy. Consider a world defined by just *two* spatial dimensions; a flat plane of zero thickness, where everything exists in x and y but not in z. What I'm saying is nobody can move or perceive anything above or below the plane. Imagine people drawn on a sheet of paper. Now, if you jab a pencil through it, they only see that an infinitely thin disk of wood and graphite has appeared from nowhere. It's a mystery to them because they don't know it's a cross-section of a *three* dimensional object intersecting their world. And that's how the symbols appear to us: they extend to and from other worlds, leaving an enigmatic imprint on ours.'

'So they're not really symbols at all?'

The man shook his head. 'Everybody referred to them as symbols for obvious reasons, but they're more like shadows cast by shapes whose true forms are infinitely more complex than our simian brains can envisage. In fact, the sphere's external geometry extends into myriad spatial dimensions, but just *appears* as an icosahedron to us. This unseen structure was modified by the Lyrans to create the gateways, which is another reason it still resides here.'

'So the Lyrans look at us like we look at the flat people on the paper?'

'To some extent, but they too are three-dimensional beings. The difference is they can see the pencil and have found a way of sliding along it.'

'To another sheet of paper,' Colin said.

'Correct,' the man said. 'And to the next one, and the one after that.'

'Sorry?' Wendy said.

'Other planes of existence,' Colin said. 'Running parallel to our own.'

Her reply was stifled by a loud beeping.

The man spun around and left the sphere.

Colin and Wendy followed him.

At the centre of a small black panel, high up on the wall, a green light pulsed slowly. The beeps stopped after a few seconds, and the light turned orange.

'We have to go,' he said.

Chapter Forty-four

He didn't speak until they reached the big doors. 'That alarm is one of a handful situated at key parts of the base.' He jabbed a large red button on the keypad, and the doors began to close. 'The orange light indicates the southern gateway has opened.' He strode towards the stairwell opposite the one they'd descended.

Colin and Wendy exchanged anxious glances, and then set off after him.

They took the steps two at a time.

On the walkway, he ushered them into a long, featureless corridor lit by the ubiquitous red lamps. 'Are you absolutely sure you saw nobody out there?'

'Not since leaving the reservoir,' Colin said.

'If we were followed,' Wendy said. 'We certainly weren't aware of it.'

He turned left through a pair of double doors into absolute darkness. 'You'll need your torches now.'

Three beams sliced through the gloom in quick succession.

Towering rows of thinly stocked racking made it impossible to gauge the overall size of the storeroom, but it was easily twenty feet high.

They passed at least a dozen rows before he made a sharp turn and headed down a narrow aisle. When they reached the far wall, he shone his torch at a rusty ventilation grill about eight feet from the floor.

'We'll be safe in there,' he said. 'At least for now.'

The man climbed up the racking, opened the grill and wriggled inside. Colin helped Wendy onto the racking and took a last nervous look down the aisle. He followed her inside, and then closed the grill behind them. They crawled down the galvanised ducting in single file. After about a minute, they took a right turn into a wider section. Here, they stopped and got as comfortable as they could.

'What now?' Wendy said.

'I need time to think.'

'Does this happen often?'

'Two or three times a year, although I doubt this is a routine reactor check.'

'Reactor?'

'The base is powered by a small nuclear power plant. It doesn't run continuously anymore, but, once in a while, a maintenance team come in to check it over. More often than not, they lower the fuel rods and spin the turbines for a few hours to charge the battery banks. It's sufficient for limited lighting and occasional hot water.'

'What about food and drinking water?'

'There's enough tinned and dried stuff to keep me going for a few years yet, the water filtration system is very robust and the toilets still flush into the reservoir.'

'I take it you've hid in here before?'

'If I'm away from the admin block and the alarm sounds.'

'Why do you sleep up there?'

'They never go into that part of the base; there's nothing left of any importance.'

'But weren't people killed on that corridor?'

The man nodded.

'Doesn't that bother you?'

'In a strange way, it makes me feel less alone. It's a gruesome but nevertheless tangible connection with flesh and blood humanity.'

Wendy frowned. 'I hadn't thought of it like that.'

Colin looked into the man's eyes. 'Can I ask you a straight question?'

'Be my guest.'

'Why didn't you wait for the dust to settle and escape through one of the gateways?'

'I was injured in the fire fight; caught some shrapnel in my thigh. I managed to get out and hide in the woods for a few days, but I could barely walk and the wound became infected. My only option was to self-medicate before it got serious. Under cover of darkness, I slipped back into the base and purloined the necessary antibiotics and pain killers from the medical centre. The leg took the best part of a year to heal; however, by the time I was fit enough to reach the reservoir, the gateways weren't safe. I made three attempts, but, each time, somebody appeared at the entrance before I was halfway along the passageway. I was lucky to get away without being seen. They always searched the base straight after and must've put it down to a malfunction when they didn't find me. Consequently, I made a concerted effort to seek another way out of here – '

'Who are *they* exactly?'

'Sorry?'

'If the people behind the coup were renegades, who's maintaining the base now?

'I imagine one of the more shadowy government departments.'

'Wouldn't they be sympathetic to your circumstances?'

'In this business, the line between the good guys and bad guys is blurred and anything but straight. With what I know, it wouldn't be in their interest to release me into the wider community. And that's putting it as euphemistically as I can.'

Colin frowned and nodded. 'I see … '

'Anyway,' the man said. 'As I was saying – I scoured every nook and cranny, every piece of ducting I could crawl into. I'd just about given up when I stumbled on something in the admin block that afforded an unexpected insight, namely a set of drawings of the entire base; some dating back to the original installation. There are several ventilation outlets, but they're quite narrow and inaccessible from the inside; however, when I superimposed one of the newer drawings over an original, I spotted a duct close to a natural fissure not shown on the later one. I found the location and managed to remove a panel with nothing more than a spanner and a hacksaw. But it didn't go too well after that: the fissure was there alright, but blocked by boulders that took several weeks to clear. Then, when I squeezed through, I found myself staring down a fifty foot, sheer drop – so close, and yet so far.'

'Is there no rope in the base?' Colin said.

'I didn't look.'

'Why not?'

'I'm terrified of heights. I ventured up there on a number of occasions to get some fresh air and grapple with my acrophobia, but it was no use. I returned to the drawings, scrutinising them for hours on end in a fruitless search for another option. Einstein once said that insanity is doing the same thing over and over again and expecting a different outcome. I can wholeheartedly concur with him.'

'So there's no other way out?' Wendy said.

The man shook his head. 'The original access points are sealed with huge rock slabs only copious amounts of dynamite would clear.'

'Can we get to the fissure from here?' Colin said.

The man nodded. 'But it's too high, even if you're unaffected by heights.'

'I'd still like to see for myself.'

The man shook his head. 'I wouldn't build your hopes.'

'What's the alternative?' Wendy said.

He sighed. 'If they know you're here, there isn't one.'

Chapter Forty-five

They crawled for a further twenty yards and stopped at a rusty, circular hatch set into the roof. The man twisted the creaky handle and tugged it open. Colin shone his torch up the shaft, but the beam didn't reach the top.

'Mind how you go on the ladder,' the man said. 'It's quite narrow.'

They climbed for around thirty feet into another duct, and then made a bewildering succession of right and left turns through a maze of intersections.

After around ten minutes, they arrived at another T-junction, but it was plain to see they'd reached their destination: a large panel had been removed from the opposite wall and placed on the floor a few feet away.

Their torch beams scanned the rough grey rock.

The man edged towards it and beckoned to Colin. 'You have to get between the rock and the ducting with your feet planted on the edge of this panel. It's a bit of a squeeze, but the fissure is easy to get into after that.'

With a little help, Colin removed his rucksack and eased through the opening. The rock rasped against his jacket and trousers as he straightened up, and he winced when a shaft of sunlight sliced into his eyes. He took a deep breath of the crisp air and peered into the fissure. It was roughly triangular in shape, about four feet wide at the bottom and six tall. It was difficult to judge distance, but he estimated it to be five or six yards deep.

'I'm going through now,' he said.

'We're right behind you,' the man said.

Colin climbed into the fissure and crept towards the light. He crouched down at the edge and took in the view over the reservoir.

Serried ranks of conifers marched down the steep, furrowed slopes to a swathe of glinting grey water. Low rain clouds brooded over the surrounding fells.

The drop didn't look as high as the man had claimed: more like thirty feet than fifty. But it was somewhat academic with no visible hand or foot holds in the vertical cliff face.

Wendy approached, and he shuffled sideways to make room for her.

'Fresh air feels good,' she said. 'Is that Raven Crag over there?'

'I think it must be – we lost some altitude in the base, but I reckon we're at least half a mile south of the gateway.'

'There or thereabouts,' the man said from behind.

'There *has* to be a way down,' Colin said. 'We can't be more than twenty minutes from the reservoir, and the woods will give us cover.'

She leaned over the edge. 'Any ideas?'

Colin stared at the Gore-Tex logo on her sleeve. 'Your jacket and rucksack; they're both good quality.'

'The best I could afford. What're you getting at?'

'Tied together with mine, we've got a makeshift rope that *might* be long enough and strong enough.'

She nodded. 'It's worth a try.'

The man turned around. 'I'll go back and get your rucksacks.'

'I'll give you a hand,' she said.

Chapter Forty-six

Spare clothing from the rucksacks added much needed length, but tying jacket sleeves and trouser legs to shoulder straps and belts wasn't as straightforward as Colin had envisaged, and the first attempts couldn't withstand a hefty tug. The man returned to the duct with Wendy's Swiss army knife and stripped a fistful of thick cables from a junction box. Wound tight around the knots, they provided additional strength and cured the slipping problem.

Colin lowered the ponderous chain and peered over the edge. 'I reckon it's ten feet shy of the bottom, which means we've got a drop of five to six feet.'

'That's not too bad,' Wendy said. 'But haven't we missed something?

'Like what?' Colin said.

'How do we secure it at this end?'

He scanned the fissure. 'Fuck's sake! There must be *something* we can hook it onto.'

'There's no need,' the man said. 'If you go first, we can take your weight up here, and I can manage the lady on my own.'

'What about you?' she said.

'I'm staying here.'

'But you – '

'It's the only way you'll get down, and I'd panic if I went anywhere near the edge.'

Wendy's eyes met Colin's. 'What do you think?'

He chewed his lip. 'It does make sense.'

She turned to the man. 'What'll happen to you?'

He shrugged. 'If they find me, and that's highly likely now, they'll extract all I know one way or

195

another, but I shouldn't worry; I don't even know your names, and the information you gave me is fascinating but not enough to track you down. After that, I imagine I'll be disposed of.' He flashed a fragile smile. 'I'd resigned myself to dying alone in here. My biggest fear was that I'd succumb to a terminal disease and have to take matters into my own hands when the morphine expired. At least, this way, it'll be over quickly.'

'Jesus Christ,' Wendy whispered.

'Your stoicism is admirable,' Colin said. 'But I've given you enough to put them on my scent.'

The man narrowed his eyes. 'A burnt out factory and a dodgy helmet cobbled together by a man forty years dead; I'd say it's a long shot.'

'I agree,' she said. 'They won't find you with *that*.'

Colin glared at Wendy. He wanted to remind her that Cranshaw had been mentioned: where UFOs were seen hovering over said burnt out factory on the day of the power surge, where the local police had the other helmet *and* his details on file. But saying that now would make matters ten times worse.

'You have to go,' the man said. 'Time isn't on your side.'

'And I'm getting cold,' she said.

Colin took a deep breath. 'Okay, let's do it.'

The man reached into his parka. 'There's something I want you to have.' He pulled out a small notebook and handed it to him. 'I don't know what you plan to do after today, but you need to read this before you decide.'

Colin slipped it into his trouser pocket. 'If we get out of here in one piece, I'll take you up on that.' He lowered the makeshift rope and passed the end to Wendy. She and the man got into position and signalled

196

they were ready. Colin gripped a rucksack strap and lowered himself over the edge. His boots found the rock, but, as he braced himself to step off, the rope slipped. It was only a couple of feet, but it felt like ten.

His heart leapt, and a cold shudder shot up his spine.

'Sorry!' Wendy shouted. 'We've got you now!'

You better fucking have!

He took a couple of deep breaths and resumed his descent.

When he reached the last jacket, he lowered himself as a far as he could and let go. He landed painlessly, but he slipped on the loose scree and jarred his wrist on a jagged boulder.

He rubbed the joint and looked up at the fissure.

Wendy was leaning over the edge, giving him the thumbs up.

He returned the gesture and waited for her to get into position on the rope.

He shouted instructions about where to put her feet, but they were largely ignored, and she descended without trouble.

When she reached the bottom, he put his hands on her waist and helped her down.

'Have you climbed before?' he said.

'In my twenties,' she said. 'But it never really leaves you.'

'You can drop the rope now!' he shouted up at the fissure.

'Forgive me if I don't come to the edge!' the man replied.

They stepped back as the twisting chain of clothing and rucksacks hurtled towards them. It hit the ground in a succession of dull thumps, scattering small stones in all directions.

He gestured towards the nearby conifers. 'We need to get under cover.'

Wendy looked up at the fissure. 'Goodbye and good luck!'

There was no reply.

They exchanged shrugs and walked towards the makeshift rope.

They folded it up as best they could and carried it into the trees, where they reclaimed their clothing and rucksacks. There were some small tears and plenty of scuff marks, but everything was still functional.

Colin was in the process of adjusting his rucksack straps when Wendy nudged his arm and pointed through a gap in the trees.

The man was standing at the edge of the fissure, staring at the sky.

'I thought he was scared of heights,' he said.

'Terrified more like,' she said. 'He wouldn't even go near the edge.'

They watched transfixed as he lifted his arms out wide.

He held the pose for a few moments, and then fell forward.

Wendy's scream drowned the noise of impact.

Chapter Forty-seven

Wendy made towards the motionless body, but Colin caught her arm.

She spun around. 'Let go! We can't leave him like that!'

'He's dead or dying.'

She tried to tug her arm free, but he held on tight.

'Get off me!'

'What're you going to do? Administer last rites or drop a rock on his head?'

'You callous sod!'

'We need to get the fuck out of here!'

'But he – '

'If you go over there, you're on your own.'

Her fierce gaze was matched by his.

'I *mean* it, Wendy.'

A noise from above stymied her response.

The pulsing whump whump grew louder, and the air turned around them.

The dark silhouette of a helicopter hovered just above the trees.

'That settles it,' he said.

They ran into the woods.

The ground steepened quickly, and their pace slowed, but the helicopter didn't seem to be following. After around five minutes, they stopped at a narrow stream and scanned the sky. They were breathing hard, and Colin could feel sweat on his back.

'Don't think they saw us,' he gasped.

Wendy grimaced. 'I wouldn't bet on it – and I doubt we're alone in these woods.'

He surveyed the arrow straight conifers with growing unease.

Wendy reached for her water bottle and unscrewed the cap. 'How do you fancy tackling Helvellyn?'

'I don't,' he said flatly. 'Why do you ask?'

'Because, if we *have* been clocked, they'll be looking for a couple in hiking gear on *this* side of the reservoir. We need to get to the other side pronto. They're bound to widen the search area, so, if we get back to the pub from that direction, it'll create the impression we've been up there all day.'

He frowned. 'Can we get to the King's Head that way?'

She took a swig and wiped her mouth. 'There's an old pony track that leads down to the farm next door. We don't have to tackle the summit; we can cut across the high slopes and join it above the pub.'

'Sounds like a plan to me.'

'Where exactly are we now?'

Colin pulled out his phone and tapped the GPS app. 'Just need the satellite to finds us … come on, come on … fucking thing.' He studied the screen. 'Let's see … we're about a third of a mile south of Raven Crag. If we head south and cross the main road at Wythburn, we can pick up the path to Helvellyn and take it from there.'

'How far to the road?'

'Err … I reckon four miles at the most, which'll take us about three hours across this terrain.' He glanced at his watch. 'We'll be there or thereabouts at three o'clock latest, so if we allow the same again to reach the pub, we'll get back well before dark.'

'And I suggest we split up when we clear the treeline up to Helvellyn and allow half an hour between our arrival times. If they do widen the search area, we'll be easy to spot and a lone hiker shouldn't arouse suspicion.'

He nodded. 'All right, let's do it.'

The woods were deserted, but the going was more difficult than expected, and they had to tackle some steep and rocky terrain to keep within the trees. A dark grey helicopter passed low overhead at roughly fifteen minute intervals, but its business appeared to be elsewhere.

After around forty minutes, they heard an idling engine directly ahead.

They decided to climb around it and headed towards a shallow bluff of grey rock some twenty feet above. A few moments later, the sounds of voices and slamming doors stopped them in their tracks. The hubbub didn't last long, and the engine noise faded away towards the reservoir.

When they reached the bluff, a gap in the trees revealed a muddy track about thirty feet below. Deep tyre tracks stopped just in front of a sheer rock wall.

Colin turned to Wendy. 'Must be the other gateway.'

She nodded. 'Can't be anything else.'

They rounded the feature and continued in silence at a more measured pace.

As they approached the southern tip of the reservoir, the trees thinned out, leaving no option but to cross the narrow tarmac road and follow the wooded shoreline.

It was nearly quarter to three when they clambered over a dry stone wall and dashed across the A591 towards the steep forest path.

They stopped at the treeline for a much needed rest and consulted their maps.

Wendy traced out a route that hugged the contours around Helvellyn's bleak slopes and met the old pony track about half a mile from the pub. As an added precaution, they swapped rucksacks to further confuse any pursuers.

She adjusted her rucksack straps. 'I won't call unless there's a problem.'

He gave the thumbs up. 'See you in the bar. Mine's a pint.'

She smiled and returned the thumbs up. 'It'll have your name on it.'

She scanned the grey sky through narrowed eyes, and then set off.

He watched her climb for a few minutes, and then sat down on a fallen tree.

Half an hour into his climb, he noticed two dark specks circling Raven Crag. After a couple of minutes, one descended into the trees, and the other headed south.

Within another half hour, the weather closed in, bringing sporadic rain on a stiff northerly wind. By the time he found the pony track, dark clouds hid the sun, and the temperature had dropped markedly. As he made his descent towards the pub, the glowing windows spurred him on and took his mind off the chill creeping into his bones.

When he reached the car park, a rumble of thunder resounded over the western fells, and his phone rang. Wendy's name glowed on the screen.

'Hi,' he said. 'Everything okay?'

'Where are you now?'

'Just got to the car park.'

'Don't go in the pub!'

'Walking away now. What's up?'

'There're two plain clothes policemen in the lounge. They stopped me before I got to reception.'

'Go on.'

'They said a body had been found in the woods around Thirlmere and wanted to know if I'd seen anything suspicious. They said it was male, possibly a vagrant, and they were treating it as suspicious for reasons they couldn't disclose. I said I'd been up Helvellyn all day, but then they started asking questions about you. They know we arrived in your car and left together this morning.'

'Shit!'

'Exactly, but I think I've got us off the hook if we get our story straight. I told them we're having an affair, and I was trying to be discreet.'

'So where did you say I was?'

'I said we'd had a row about telling your wife, and I stormed off without you.'

He scanned the car park. 'Okay. Anything else?'

'We met on line three months ago when I was shopping for hiking gear. They asked why we were booked into separate rooms, but I told them I wasn't under caution and to mind their own business.'

'Is that it?'

'Only that we left the pub after breakfast and took the pony track up to the summit. And I gave them our real names because they must've checked the guest list with reception.'

'Right then, I'll make my entrance and act all surprised when they stop me.'

'Stick to the story, and you'll be fine.'

'I'll come to your room when we're through.'

'One more thing,' she said. 'I don't think they're real detectives.'

'Why do you say that?'

'This is all happening way too quickly. He would've lain there for weeks, maybe longer, before anybody found him.'

'Good point. It isn't easy to get up there without a helicopter.'

'Just bear it in mind.'

'Will do.'

He ended the call and walked towards the pub.

When he entered, two smartly dressed men rose from their armchairs.

One was tall and bald, the other squat with greying hair and a thick moustache.

There was nobody else around.

The bald man smiled at him and flashed a warrant card. 'Good evening, sir. I'm Detective Sergeant Wilcox and this is Detective Constable Hewitt.'

Colin removed his beanie and slipped off Wendy's rucksack. 'How can I help you?'

'Could you tell us your name?'

'Colin Thurcroft. Address and car registration at reception.'

'Thank you, Mr Thurcroft,' DS Wilcox said. 'We're here on a routine enquiry about a body that was found in the woods around Thirlmere earlier today.'

Colin mustered a solemn expression. 'Okay ... '

DS Wilcox recounted the details he'd heard from Wendy, and then asked if he had any information that might help.

'I wish I had,' Colin said. 'But I've been walking Helvellyn all day.'

'Alone?'

'Why do you ask?'

'We've already spoken to Wendy Cooper.'

'Then you know why we're here.'

'We'd like to hear it from you.'

'Let's just say my wife has no idea I'm with Wendy.'

'I couldn't help noticing you're booked into separate rooms.'

'Where is this going?'

'Bear with me, Mr Thurcroft.'

Colin sighed. 'My wife thinks I'm up here on business, Detective. She helps with the bookkeeping, and this way it doesn't look suspicious when the credit card statement arrives.'

Brilliant!

'How long have you known her?'

'Wendy or my wife?'

DS Wilcox frowned. 'I thought that would be obvious.'

'Just a few months.'

'You set off together this morning, but *she* got back fifteen minutes ago.'

'Let's just say we had a disagreement about commitment.'

DS Wilcox nodded. 'I understand, Mr Thurcroft.'

Both men stared at Colin, and an awkward silence ensued.

'Is there anything else?' Colin said.

'No, I don't think so. Thanks for your cooperation.'

Wendy opened the bedroom door and beckoned Colin inside. 'How did it go?'

He dropped her rucksack next to his. 'Hard to say – there was a little too much interest in our relationship for my taste.'

'Like they doubted we were actually *in* one.'

'That's the vibe I got.'

'They *can't* be real coppers, can they?'

'I doubt it, which means he was in clear view of the helicopter when he jumped.'

'Creating a timely distraction for us.'

He ran his fingers through his hair. 'I hadn't thought of it like that … '

She squeezed his arm. 'Sorry I lost my temper when you pulled me back. If you hadn't, we'd have been in deep shit.'

'We wouldn't have reached the road, Wendy.'

She plonked onto the bed and sighed. 'I don't think any of it has sunk in yet.'

'Hardly surprising when you consider what we've been through.'

He went to the rain-speckled window and gazed at the bruised sky.

'Do you think we've slipped the net?' she said.

He shrugged. 'I don't know what's going on, to be honest. They obviously know *somebody* entered the base, and they're actively trying to find them. That said, if we were actually seen at the boulder, they'd have a good description, and the bogus Bobbies would've felt our collars.'

'I doubt we'd have even got into the base.'

He frowned. 'Good point.'

'I don't think we were seen, Colin – call it female intuition, but I'm pretty sure we were alone up there. We probably triggered some sort of alarm at the boulder. So they know the base was entered and the intruder must've been complicit in the scientist's death, but that'll likely be all they have. I imagine they're checking the nearby hotels and hostels on the off chance somebody might've seen something.'

'You might be right.'

They didn't speak for a few moments.

'So what do we do now?' she said.

'Get out of here sharpish tomorrow.' He slipped the man's notebook from his pocket. 'And find a place to study without interruption.'

She smiled. 'I'd forgotten about that.'

'I leafed through some of it when I was waiting to set off after you.'

'And?'

'His handwriting's hard to read, and there's a lot of unintelligible techie stuff, but I gleaned enough to know the base wasn't closed; it was relocated.'

'That doesn't surprise me.'

'Nor me.'

'Did he say where?'

'Not yet.'

'He never got to tell us why it all ended so violently, did he?'

'No, but it'll be interesting to find out.'

'So we're not going to let this drop?'

'Not just yet,' he said. 'Let's see how we feel when we know more.'

'Fair enough.'

'And for the rest of our stay, we need to behave like any normal cheating couple.'

'Really?' She flashed an impish wink. 'What did you have in mind?'

He blushed. 'You *know* what I – '

'Sorry, Colin, but you walked into that.'

Their eyes met, but the words he craved refused to form, and the moment was gone.

Shit! Shit! Shit!

She smiled warmly. 'Let's get cleaned up and go down to the bar.'

He grabbed his rucksack and went to the door. 'How long do you need?'

'I'll give you a knock in an hour.'

'Don't leave it any longer,' he said. 'I'm bloody starving!'

Chapter Forty-eight

Wendy opened the glove box and rummaged through the crammed contents.

Colin pulled out of the King's Head car park and gunned the engine. 'I've stayed there a couple of times when I've been up here on business.'

She found the hotel leaflet and scanned it quickly. 'Hmm … looks okay to me.'

'Should be there in an hour or so.'

She yawned. 'Can we stop off in Ambleside?'

'If you want – '

'I need some cash and a tube of travel wash.'

'That's not a bad idea,' he said. 'And I could check out the competition.'

They left the car in the Rydal Road car park and strolled into the town. At the traffic lights on Compston Road, they decided to split up and meet half an hour later back at the car. Colin withdrew some money at an ATM, and then perused the shops.

Ambleside was a shopping hotspot for outdoor gear, and he made at least three visits a year to get a feel for what was selling and what wasn't.

He lost track of time, chatting with shop staff, and returned to the car ten minutes late.

Wendy was nowhere to be seen.

He tried her mobile, but it went straight to voicemail.

He strolled up and down for a couple of minutes. When it started to rain, he got into the car and switched on the radio. He drummed the steering wheel and told himself nothing was wrong, that she was trying something on and had forgotten the time, or she'd nipped to the public toilet, or something else he couldn't think of at the moment. His frustration turned to anxiety as the minutes ticked by.

After another two attempts to phone her, he left the car and strode back into town.

He checked all the popular cafes and shops. On one occasion, he thought he'd spotted her, but he almost cried out when the woman turned around to reveal somebody considerably older and probably Chinese.

Thirty five minutes later, he returned to the car park.

His heart thumped wildly, and he could taste the breakfast bacon again.

In desperation, he scanned the rows of cars, but there was no sign of her.

God Almighty, Wendy! Where the fuck are you?

He took a few hurried breaths to thwart the rising panic, but it had little effect. She'd been gone for too long now and there was no innocent explanation for it. The only thing he could do was to return to the car, pull himself together and consider his options.

When he opened the driver's door, somebody grabbed his arm.

Wendy!

He spun around, but the fierce blue eyes weren't hers.

'Do as I say and you won't get hurt.' The man raised the handgun. 'The car keys.'

Colin was too shocked to be frightened.

He dropped the keys into his palm.

His assailant was blonde, no older than forty and dressed in hiking gear.

'Get in and move over to the passenger side.'

Colin regained some composure.

'Look, mate, I don't know what you – '

The man opened his mouth, but no words formed. He shuddered violently and collapsed like a discarded rag doll.

Another man stood in his place.

Dark, impassive eyes met Colin's through thick-rimmed glasses under a creased brow and neat, side-parted hair. He wore a beige mackintosh over a white shirt and black tie.

'Please get in, Mr Thurcroft,' he said in a refined accent. 'We haven't much time.'

Colin felt his willpower implode. Without hesitation, he did as instructed and watched numbly as the man, a dead ringer for his old history teacher, prised the keys and handgun from the blonde man's rigid fingers. He yanked the body away from the car with disquieting ease and shut the driver's door.

Colin gripped the steering wheel until his knuckles turned white.

The man opened the passenger door and got in.

He offered the keys. 'Leave the car park and turn left.'

Colin started the engine and selected reverse.

His actions felt oddly detached, almost as if he was watching himself from a distance.

They travelled in silence through the sluggish traffic.

After a minute or so, Colin roused from his trancelike state.

'The man in the car park,' he said. 'Did you kill him?'

'Electrically stunned.'

'Where's Wendy?'

'She was abducted, as you would've been if I hadn't intervened.'

'By who?'

'This isn't the time or place to answer that question.'

'What will they do to her?'

'I reiterate my last statement, but, rest assured, they want her alive.'

'Why?'

The man's voice hardened. 'Concentrate on the road and listen for my directions.'

They were about a mile from Ambleside when he spoke again.

'Turn left here.'

They drove onto a narrow stone bridge over a stream.

'Turn right and stop at the side of the cattle grid.'

Colin did as instructed and switched off the engine.

The man, he'd decided to call *Mackintosh*, unbuckled his seatbelt. 'In the circumstances, I intend to keep this as succinct as possible, Mr Thurcroft. You are about to be transported to a safe house, where you will be debriefed about your recent activities. In the meantime, wheels will be set in motion to allow you to return home and resume your life.'

'Just like that?'

'You are not the focus of attention.'

'But Wendy *is*?'

'Most definitely.'

'And who or what do you represent?'

Mackintosh reached into his inside pocket and pulled out a phone. He tapped the screen twice and stared straight ahead. 'I shall provide what insight I can when I have debriefed you.'

Chapter Forty-nine

A black Volvo S60 approached at speed. It rattled over the cattle grid and stopped alongside them. A bald, stocky man, in a dark fleece and black cargo trousers, got out of the front passenger door and flexed his shoulders.

Mackintosh held out his hand. 'The car keys and your mobile phone, Mr Thurcroft.'

Colin reached into his jacket and slid the keys from the ignition.

When they got out of the car, Mackintosh gestured at the rear door of the Volvo. 'Quick as you can.'

Colin got in and watched distractedly as Mackintosh passed his keys to the bald man, and then got into the front passenger seat. The driver pulled off and turned onto the narrow lane leading away from the bridge.

'Fasten your seatbelt,' Mackintosh said. 'It will be an hour or so before we reach our destination.'

Colin found the buckle and inserted the shaky metal tongue at the second attempt.

He glanced at the door mirror and saw his own car close behind with the bald man at the wheel.

Mackintosh made occasional and barely audible small talk with the driver, which left him alone with his troubled thoughts.

He'd already decided to tell him everything, but he wanted answers too. And Wendy was uppermost in his mind. Why was *she* the focus of attention? What did she have that was so important? He racked his memory for anything she'd said that might provide a clue, but nothing came to light. It had to be something to do with her father, but that was a long time ago, and she knew very little about his life before he left the states. Or so she said.

His thoughts drifted until he remembered how the man in the base had reacted when she told him who she was, and that he'd asked her if she was an only child. Is that why he'd given him the notebook? Would that provide the insight? He had to finish reading it, but it was in the sports bag in his car, and they'd probably search his belongings when they got to wherever they were going. There was nothing to be done now, but he knew he'd have to think on his feet when the time came.

He leaned back and watched the countryside race by his window.

Now the sense of loss hit him. It was as if it had been waiting in the wings for the right moment, and this was it. His suppressed and unrequited feelings broke free and rushed him with an emotional torrent that threatened to break his fragile composure.

He met the driver's cold stare in the rear view mirror, and looked away.

He took a few deep breaths and wiped his eyes.

They re-joined the main road at the Waterhead ferry landing, and headed towards Windermere. They turned off at Staveley and dashed along a succession of rolling lanes. By the time they reached the A685, Colin was feeling car sick. The wider, smoother road settled his stomach and, within five minutes, converged on the M6 motorway and shadowed it north towards Tebay. They passed through the village and continued east until they reached Ravenstonedale. Here, they turned onto a narrow lane which climbed gently into the nearby hills. After several sharp turns, Colin lost all sense of direction and regained his car sickness. Just when he thought he'd have to ask them to pull over, they reached their destination.

The nondescript, two-storey house nestled into the grassy hillside against a clutch of wind-twisted Scots Pines. Iron grey stone walls merged with the steep slate roof to create a giant tombstone in Colin's anxiety-riddled mind.

Another black S60 was parked on the roadside.

It flashed its headlights and sped away.

Colin's car passed by and drove through the rusty gates. When it was out of sight behind the house, they followed and parked on the muddy driveway.

He glanced at his watch. It was ten past twelve.

When they got out, he assessed the driver properly. Like the bald man, he was well built, but with a thinner face and short ginger hair. He wore a beige sports jacket over a white shirt and faded jeans.

Mackintosh led the way to the back door, where the bald man waited with the luggage and rucksacks from Colin's car.

The musty kitchen's cheap, wood-veneered units; ancient gas cooker; and greasy, floral tiles reminded him of his old student digs.

The driver went upstairs, and the other two began to search through the sports bags on the solid wood table. When the bald man found the notebook, he flicked through it and handed it to Mackintosh.

He studied a few pages at random and turned to Colin. 'Where did you get this?'

'It was given to me,' he said. 'By a dead man in Area 62.'

The bald man stopped searching, and both of them stared at Colin.

Mackintosh cleared his throat. 'Take off your jacket and shoes, Mr Thurcroft.' He gestured towards an open door. 'And then go through to the lounge. I shall join you presently.'

The room was sparsely furnished with a tatty wood framed suite and a sideboard that might've been liberated from a skip. There was no television or ornaments of any kind; charred holes peppered the threadbare carpet where it met the sooty fireplace; and dark green curtains and a sagging pelmet squeezed the meagre light from the grimy window. The musty smell was much stronger than in the kitchen.

Colin sat down in an armchair facing the window.

Mackintosh entered and shut the door. He took off his eponymous coat and draped it over the sofa. 'Excuse the rather disagreeable setting, but we choose properties for specific reasons and rarely use them more than once.' He sat down and crossed his legs. 'From now on, you may refer to me as Anderson.'

I preferred Mackintosh ...

'Not your real name, I assume.'

'I'm not at liberty to say, but I find anonymity a hindrance in these situations.'

'Situations where you need information from an abductee.'

'If you like.'

'I don't intend to hold back. I'll tell you everything I know, then you tell me what's happened to Wendy, then we go our separate ways. That's how it works, yeah?'

'Providing I'm satisfied you haven't withheld information.'

Colin frowned. 'I'll do my best.'

'Right then,' Anderson said. 'Let's start at the beginning, shall we?

'Okay … it all started when I decided to buy a retail outlet for my online business – '

'Outdoor clothing, isn't it?'

'How much do you already know?'

'I've done my homework, but I need you to fill in the blanks and join the dots.'

'The property was derelict, but I badgered the local council to push through a compulsory purchase order. It all seemed to be going well until we got in there and found – '

A knock at the door cut him short.

'Come,' Anderson said.

The bald man entered with the plastic bag containing the helmet and spoke for the first time. 'Thought you'd want to see this, sir.'

Anderson reached inside and pulled it out.

He held it up to the light, and then turned to the bald man. 'You can leave us now.'

He did as requested and shut the door behind him.

'Well now,' Anderson said. 'What have we here?'

Colin sighed. 'As I was saying … '

He recounted everything without interruption.

When he'd finished, Anderson thanked him and went into the kitchen to organise hot drinks.

He returned with two mugs and a packet of digestive biscuits under his arm.

Colin took a mug and a couple of biscuits. He dipped one in his coffee and popped it into his mouth. He hadn't realised how hungry he was.

Anderson took a sip and rested his mug on the arm of the sofa. 'Is there anything you've missed or want to expand upon?'

Colin shook his head. 'Err – no, I don't think so.'

'If anything does spring to mind, let me know.'

'Will do.'

'Now, I would assume you have some questions for me.'

'One or two.'

'Understand that I may only be able to answer them in part or not at all.'

'My overriding concern is Wendy.'

'As is mine, albeit for quite different reasons.'

'What reasons?'

'Her father wasn't your average, run-of-the-mill boffin, Mr Thurcroft; he was, by all accounts, a bona fide genius in his field.'

'Which was?'

'Genetics,' Anderson said. 'The acquisition of the first sphere gave the US team a head start over everybody else. At the time of his departure, they were easily twenty years ahead of the most advanced mainstream research.'

'I was led to believe the genetic experiments only started after the failed escape attempt at Thirlmere.'

'Not so. The Oregon crew were injured in the rather bumpy landing, and, before they regenerated, a small sample of cerebral tissue was surreptitiously acquired. Unbeknown to our visitors, a separate installation was commissioned just to study it, but genetic research was in its infancy and little was learned. The situation changed dramatically soon after her father was recruited in 1964. Under his direction, a remarkable amount of progress was made; however, at some point, he had a change of heart and turned against the project. Ms Cooper told you about the meeting with Klein and his speedy exit when his activities became known, but this is not the full story. Before he left, he started a fire which destroyed key parts of the installation and all the project records.'

'That's some change of heart.'

'Best guess: he wanted Klein's help to leak the information in a controlled manner. When that backfired, he resorted to a far more drastic contingency plan.'

'Sounds like he'd been planning this for some time?'

'Undoubtedly,' Anderson said. 'And he didn't leave empty handed.'

'Go on.'

'He stole a crucial piece of modified genetic material that is still desperately sought.'

'Namely?'

'The hybrid you know as Wendy Cooper.'

Chapter Fifty

Colin stared open-mouthed at Anderson.

'I did wonder if it was wise to tell you this, but, at the end of the day, I thought it might help you to appreciate the gravity of the situation.'

He blew out his cheeks. 'It's done that all right.'

'It may be some consolation to know that she was almost certainly unaware of it.'

'Why did he save her?'

'The modified egg, placed in the womb of a surrogate volunteer, was fertilised with his own sperm.'

'So he *was* her real father?'

'Yes, he was,' Anderson said. 'A situation which must have made her dissection all the more unpalatable.'

'They were going to cut her up?'

Anderson nodded. 'Shortly after her second birthday, she was subjected to a battery of tests that uncovered some unusual mental abilities and – '

'In particular?' Colin said.

'Why do you ask?'

'She said she sometimes saw people that weren't actually there.'

'Did she communicate with them?'

'No, but she thought they wanted to talk to her. She said she saw a man with long hair and dark eyes standing behind me at Ilfracombe harbour.'

Anderson frowned. 'It would be rash to speculate without more information, but I can say that her enhanced occipital lobe allowed some perception of other realities.'

'But she struggled to see the symbol on the rock … '

'That did surprise me when you first mentioned it.'

'Not until I traced out the triangle, anyway.'

'Then she saw it?'

'Yeah, I remember her saying so.'

'That wouldn't be possible for a normal person without the cerebral stimulation you employed. One only sees the rock collapse in on itself to form the gateway.'

'What else was different about her?'

'She has some telepathic and telekinetic abilities.'

Colin felt a flush of heat on his neck. 'She kept that quiet.'

'The telekinesis was something of a surprise as the Lyrans didn't possess that particular capability, but I doubt she was aware of her ability to move objects remotely. From what I can gather, the telepathy would only allow her to hear what someone was saying a fraction of a second before they actually formed the words.'

Colin shook his head. 'Jesus H … '

'As I was saying, they planned to monitor her closely until puberty when it was deemed apposite to dissect the brain. What they learned would set the platform for phase two, which was to produce a batch of improved hybrids to study more extensively. But the fire put paid to all that. It was difficult to control in an underground base, especially with a sabotaged sprinkler system. Nobody died, but the survivors soon realised how much of the gene splicing know-how he'd kept to himself, and how much disinformation he'd sown over the course of the project.'

'Did they find out who'd tipped him off?'

Anderson shook his head and reached for his mug.

Colin frowned. 'But surely the ground has been made up by now. We were told, in the base, that successful human hybrids were created there.'

'It depends what you mean by *successful*. The splicing worked, but the end results were crude compared to Ms Cooper. It seems highly likely that her father stumbled on something, quite by accident, which produced the breakthrough. Also, the genetic material acquired in 1951 was of a superior quality than that recovered from the badly charred bodies in 1975. Hence the extant interest in her.'

'So they could still cut her up?'

'Highly unlikely,' Anderson said. 'There have been significant advances since the early 1970s, which obviate such a drastic procedure.'

'And would she fare any better if *you* found her?'

'We would need a variety of tissue samples and a detailed study of her mental abilities, but that shouldn't prohibit the pursuit of a relatively normal life, and her cooperation would be amply rewarded.'

'How long have you known it was her?'

Anderson glanced at his watch. 'You supplied final confirmation about fifteen minutes ago. We didn't even know her father had settled in this country.'

'So how did you home in on us?'

'We've guarded and maintained the base since The Group left some eight years ago. You were observed at the northern gateway.'

'And the two men at the King's Head?'

'I can confirm they weren't real police officers, and they don't work for me. It would seem The Group was two steps ahead of us.'

'How did they manage that?'

'How indeed. A question I need to answer with considerable alacrity.'

'They must've known who we were before we left this morning.'

'There can be little doubt that a positive identification was made in the hotel. We don't know how at present, but her father didn't manage to destroy absolutely everything: photographs of Ms Cooper as a child survived the fire, and software is available that can match facial features from toddlers to old age. A hidden camera would have facilitated this process. Also, if they procured your details from reception, it's quite possible that your mobile phone conversations were monitored. Anyhow, once they were sure, it was just a matter of how and when they got hold of you.'

'Did *you* know we were at the King's Head?'

Anderson nodded. 'We tracked you back there.'

'So why didn't you intervene sooner?'

'The decision was made to observe your subsequent activities in the hope that you would lead us to The Group's location or, at least, a senior operative.'

'You thought we were working for *them*?'

'Who else would have known how to enter the base?'

Colin sighed. 'Fair point.'

They sipped their drinks in silence.

Colin spoke first. 'How much can you tell me about yourself and the organisation you represent?'

'Nothing about myself, I'm afraid, but the organisation I toil for is part of Her Majesty's Civil Service, although not one you would find officially listed.'

'And what was your involvement with The Group?'

'The tortuous history of The Group's relationship with national governments is classified. However, the salient points regarding the dramatic events at the base are already known to you, so I can confirm that a renegade element did take control and eliminated all opposition within its ranks. Unbeknown to us, or our American and Russian counterparts, they had been planning this for some time. Apparently, it was meant to be a bloodless coup, but somebody in the UK base got wind of what they were up to, and things got out of hand. Regrettably, they managed to conceal it from us until they had scarpered.'

'Where did they go?'

'Even if I knew, I wouldn't be at liberty to say. Their vanishing act was most impressive, and, even with the considerable resources available to us, we haven't been able to locate them.'

'What about the people who kidnapped Wendy? Didn't you follow them?'

'Indeed we did, but they were ready for us. One of my operatives is dead and another seriously injured.'

Colin frowned. 'What do they mean to achieve?'

'They have a grand design founded in a misguided and truly heinous premise, but that's all I can tell you.'

They didn't speak for a few moments.

Anderson glanced at his watch. 'I think that concludes the debrief.'

'What happens now?'

'We wait.'

'Sorry?'

'The metaphoric wheels I mentioned earlier need chance to turn.'

'How do you mean?'

'The man you encountered in the car park wasn't alone. His colleague was apprehended and taken to another safe house. He has since been released with instructions that you are of no further use to either party.'

'And they'll go for that?'

'They may watch you for a week or two, but there's no reason to believe they will want to make contact. They have their prize. As a precaution, you and your family will be under our covert protection until the dust has settled.'

'Are you saying you'll let him go to save my skin?'

'He's a low-level operative in a cellular command structure and knows nothing about the organisation he ultimately works for. Turning him would be of little, if any, practical use, and we know from past experience that surveillance would be unproductive. The people who took Ms Cooper are a different matter, but, as you now know, they have slipped the net.'

'What's the real reason for letting me go?'

'I've just explained it to you.'

'I think you know what I'm getting at.'

'We are not gangsters, Mr Thurcroft.'

'That's not what I was – '

'The ethical argument aside, disposing of people who know too much isn't as straightforward as books and movies often imply. The repercussions can exacerbate the problem in ways that are difficult to contain.'

'So you trust me to keep schtum?'

'Trust doesn't come into it. You must not discuss this with *anybody*, not another living soul, or make any record, hard copy or otherwise, of what you know. Once you have had time to reflect on the consequences of indiscretion, you will realise there is nothing to be gained and much to lose.'

'Go on.'

'Without recourse to hyperbole, I can affirm that nothing less than the fate of humanity now hangs in the balance. On a more personal note: Ms Cooper's life depends on your cooperation in this matter, and you must also consider the swift and ruthless smear campaign that would pour scorn on any disclosure which came to our eager attention. If that was not enough, termination would be inevitable.'

Colin swallowed hard. 'Okay, I think that's clear enough.'

'At the moment, there is nothing more you can do for us; however, in appreciation of your co-operation, I have already arranged for a government department to accept your bid for an overseas contract which should double your turnover.'

'Hush money.'

'I wouldn't have phrased it quite so crudely.'

'Nevertheless … '

'Take it or leave it,' Anderson said curtly. 'You are under no obligation.'

'I'll give it some thought.'

Anderson stood up and grabbed his coat and the helmet. 'I have to leave now, but I shall return this evening.'

'There is one last thing I'd like to ask.'

'Yes?'

'The man we met in the base. Do you know his name?'

'Your description fits a particular individual whose identity must remain classified.'

Anderson left the room and shut the door.

Colin mulled over their conversation until he heard the back door slam. He went to the window and peered through the dirty glass. The other black S60 had returned.

Anderson strode down the drive and got into the back.

It sped away before the door shut.

Over the course of the afternoon, the bald man brought him pre-packed sandwiches, hot drinks and newspapers. He browsed the articles, but even the most horrid dramas couldn't trump the very personal ones running through his mind.

At just gone six, he was asked what he wanted from a fish and chip shop.

A little over an hour later, Anderson arrived with the food.

Colin ate alone in the front room and dozed off soon after.

He was woken at midnight by the bald man and escorted upstairs to a small bedroom.

He rolled up his jacket into a makeshift pillow and curled up on the bare mattress.

When sleep eventually took him, it was punctuated by nightmares and absurd dreams, none of which he could remember in the morning.

Part Four

Beyond good and evil

Chapter Fifty-one

Tuesday, 8th April

On Anderson's instruction, Colin pulled into a layby on the outskirts of Cranshaw. The Volvo stopped close behind.

Anderson reached into his coat and offered a business card. 'Use it if you're in difficulty or to relay pertinent information.'

It was blank except for a printed mobile number.

Colin slipped it into his jacket. 'You *will* let me know what you can about Wendy?'

Anderson held out his hand. 'I shall do my best.'

They shook briefly.

'Goodbye, Mr Thurcroft.'

Anderson got out of the car and strode towards the Volvo.

A few moments later, it passed by and merged into the traffic.

As expected, the house was empty.

He scanned his mail and went upstairs to unpack.

He found his phone in a side pocket of the sports bag, and called Jan.

'Col?'

'Hi Jan. How's things?'

'Where are you?'

'Honey, I'm home.'

'You should've phoned. Holly's been frantic trying to get hold of you.'

'Sorry, but it's been hard to get a signal.'

'Where've you been? Mars?'

'Not quite.'

'She said you were in Devon before you sneaked back for more clothes.'

'I spent a few days down there, then I went up to The Lakes.'

'All right for some.'

'It gave me space to think.'

'Been doing quite a bit of that myself.'

'And?'

'I'm not going to discuss it over the phone, Col.'

'When're you back?'

'I'll see if I can get away a bit earlier – eat with Holly if you like.'

'Yeah, okay.'

'We'll talk when she's in her room, yeah?'

'I'd better get some wine.'

'Good idea.'

'Bye, Jan.'

'Bye.'

He dumped his dirty clothes in the laundry basket, and then sat on the edge of the bed and stared out of the window. On the grey horizon, ragged white clouds streamed from the dark stumps of Fiddler's Ferry power station.

The events of the last few days rushed through his mind like a waking nightmare.

He fought his emotions with deep breaths, but, when the tears came, he curled up on the bed and cried like a baby.

The reunion with Holly lifted his spirits. When she'd gone to bed, he talked and drank wine with Jan until gone eleven. They decided their marriage was worth saving, for Holly's sake more than anything. Colin agreed to forgo his interest in Eric's sudden death and put all his effort s into getting the shop up and running.

They made love that night; the physical, no nonsense sort that Jan enjoyed and Colin went along with. In the afterglow, they spooned with Jan's bottom tucked into him.

He waited for her gentle snores, and then slipped out of bed.

He eased his dressing gown from the door hook, and crept towards the study.

Chapter Fifty-two

Friday, 11th April, 1.47am

Alex Jeprell stared at the busy monitor and pursed his lips. 'How long has she been in REM?'

Karen Coleridge, his most trusted technician and occasional bed partner, glanced over her spectacles at the laptop. 'Just over twenty minutes.'

'And you noticed these readings when?'

'About five minutes ago. I called you straightaway.'

Jeprell pointed at the most jagged of the waveforms. 'The occipital lobe activity is unlike anything I've ever seen.'

She nodded. 'The temporal lobe isn't too far behind.'

He rubbed his chin. 'I agree.'

'There's a distinct repetition in the waveforms every eighty-four milliseconds, but the amplitude variation seems random in both.'

'Vital signs?'

'Completely normal except for a slightly raised blood pressure.'

'Which is?'

'One-twenty over seventy-two. She averages around one-ten over sixty-five in REM.'

Jeprell turned to go. 'Keep me informed of any changes.'

'Professor?'

'Yes?'

'Can you explain this?'

He frowned. 'Best guess: she's communicating with someone.'

'Any ideas?'

The door slammed behind him.

Colin woke with a start. He wiped the cold sweat from his forehead and glanced at the radio alarm clock. The glowing red numerals read 02:36 AM. It was the third identical nightmare in as many nights, but this one had been the most vivid.

As usual, it had started in a featureless, brightly lit corridor. At the end, a heavy steel door opened slowly. He went towards it and passed through into a room girded with a bewildering collection of beeping machinery, monitors and keyboards. At the centre, wearing a blood-stained surgical gown, an unconscious Wendy was strapped into what looked like a large dentist's chair. Countless electrodes studded her shaved head, and a tangled web of tubes hung from her arms.

Colin approached, and her eyes began to flicker.

When he was just a few feet away, they opened wide.

'Colin! You came!' she cried. 'Thank God!'

He backed away. He didn't want to, but he was powerless to stop it.

She tugged and heaved at the straps. 'Where're you going? Don't leave me here!'

He desperately wanted to help but continued to retreat.

'They're going to fucking kill me!'

He was back in the corridor now.

Wendy was sobbing. 'Come back! Please, Colin … I need you … '

He turned away and found himself face to face with a smiling Anderson.

He raised a handgun to Colin's forehead. 'Well, I did warn you.'

The gun fired with a deafening roar.

Jan draped her arm over his chest. 'You awake?'
He grunted.
'Your heart's beating fast.'
'I had a bad dream.'
'What about?'
'Don't know – can't remember.'
'Roll over, and I'll rub your back.'
He did as instructed and closed his eyes.

Chapter Fifty-three

Monday, 14th April

Colin had just pulled up outside the office when his phone rang. He didn't recognise the number, but it looked familiar.

'Hello?'

'Mr Thurcroft, this is Detective Inspector Taylor. I wanted to let you know that the inquiry into Eric Manning's death is now closed, and you won't be required for any further questioning.'

'That's a relief. Thanks for the update.'

'No problem at all.'

He switched off the engine. 'There is one last thing.'

'Yeah?'

'What'll happen to the helmet Ronald Vine wanted?'

'There's been a bit of a problem on that front.'

'Go on.'

'We – err – can't seem to find it.'

'Seriously?'

'It appears to have been mislaid in the property store.'

'Right – okay – if and when it turns up, could I come and get it?'

'Providing you get permission from his sister, I don't see why not.'

'Will you let me know?'

'Of course.'

'Thanks for that.'

'No worries. Bye for now.'

'Bye.'

Colin returned the phone to his pocket and sighed.

I very much doubt it will turn up, D I Taylor.

He got out of the car and glanced down the road.

A black S60 turned the corner and parked fifty yards away.

The cemetery looked very different from the last time Colin was here. The trees teemed with budding leaves and white blossom. Bird song filled the air, and the scent of mown grass carried on the mild breeze.

He found the grave just a few yards from Eric Manning's and placed the bouquet on the heaped soil next to the solitary wreath of shrivelled chrysanthemums. According to the fresh gold inscription on the dark headstone, Ronald Vine was now "at rest" with the wife he'd lost twenty-four years ago.

He crouched down to read the message on the wreath.

His shoulder blades tingled, and he knew with absolute certainty that somebody was standing behind him.

A faint, yellow glow raced across the headstone.

He straightened up and turned around.

The breath caught in his throat.

There was nobody there.

Twenty yards away, a young woman tended a grave, and an elderly couple shuffled along the gravel path.

He ran his fingers through his hair.

Get a grip! For fuck's sake!

He crouched down again, but the writing on the sodden card was too smudged to read.

That night, he went to bed a little earlier than usual and slept without nightmares. He dreamt about Ron Vine, but it was a jumbled replay of their first conversation and only fragments survived until morning.

Chapter Fifty-four

Wednesday, 16th April

Colin parked at a cautious distance from the overfilled skip and reached for the yellow hard hat on the passenger seat. He locked the car and walked around to the front of the shop.

Inside, a cacophony of bangs and crashes resounded from above.

He surveyed the ground floor which looked much larger without the toys and shelving, and then climbed the central staircase to the second floor.

Most of the bikes had been replaced with sawn timber, stacks of plasterboard and bags of cement. The project manager was pacing up and down, talking into his phone. He gave a thumbs-up when he saw Colin and ended the call.

'Now then, Pete,' Colin said. 'How's things?'

'Okay, boss. Just chasing a skip that should've been here yesterday.'

'You couldn't get a toothpick in the one outside.'

Pete grinned. 'That's their problem now.'

'Did you talk to the architect about the new partition?'

'Yeah, he's fine with it.'

'That's a result.'

'Don't I know it?'

'So what're these notebooks you've found?'

'They're in the front room.'

Pete led the way to the top floor.

The bangs and crashes grew louder as they climbed the stairs.

He turned right in the hallway and walked through a door frame without a door, into an empty room of bare brick walls and dusty floorboards. At the centre, five neatly stacked notebooks rested on a mound of splintered wood and smashed plaster.

Colin picked up the top one and blew away the dust. 'Where did you say they were?'

'In the big bureau we took out yesterday.'

He opened it and turned the yellowed pages. 'I thought we emptied all the furniture.'

Pete went to the window. 'We did, but they were hidden behind a panel in the back.'

Colin stared at him. 'Hidden?'

'Either that, or they'd slipped down from one of the drawers.'

'So how did you find them?'

'I didn't,' Pete said. 'One of my labourers did – I know how this is going to sound, but it's like he *knew* they were there.'

'How do you mean?'

'I caught him in here a couple of times just staring at the bureau. When I asked him what he was doing, he said his grandparents used to have one the same. Then he spends his lunch break taking it apart. When he got them out, he insisted you should see them.' Pete shrugged. 'You work it out, it's beyond me.'

'Is he on site now?'

'No, he phoned in sick this morning.'

'What's up with him?'

'Migraine, apparently.'

'How old is he?'

'Why do you ask?'

Colin shrugged. 'No reason.'

'He's eighteen, I think.'

241

Thought he might be ...

'Anyway,' Pete said. 'What do you want to do with 'em?'

'I'll take them, Pete.'

Pete frowned. 'Your call – I'll go and see if I can find a plastic bag.'

Colin picked up another notebook. 'Cheers, mate.'

When he reached the fifth page, a brass Yale key slid down a list of mathematical equations and dropped onto the floorboards. He picked it up and held it to the light.

Pete returned with a bag. 'Where did you find that?'

'Inside this notebook. Why?'

'Bloody hell fire!'

'I assume you know what it's for?'

'I'll show my arse in Poundland if it doesn't open the door two down from the kitchen. It's the last room for clearing, and the key went missing two days ago.'

'The top floor doors have *never* been locked.'

Pete snorted. 'I didn't even know there were keys for them.'

'Who locked it?'

'Nobody's coughed for it, but I could hazard a guess.' He held out his hand. 'Give it here and I'll get onto it.'

Colin slipped the key into his trouser pocket. 'Hang fire for now, Pete, and go easy on him until I've had chance to look into this.'

Pete shrugged and gave him the bag. 'You're the boss.'

Alan Sharrock placed two mugs of coffee on Colin's desk and pulled up a chair.

Colin stared at his mug. 'To what do I owe the pleasure?'

'I wanted a chat now the coast is clear.'

'Why? What's up?'

'You tell me, Col.'

Colin sipped his coffee.

'You've not been yourself since you got back.'

'I'm fine, mate – just got a few things on my mind.'

Alan didn't look too convinced.

'You and Jan okay now?'

'We patched it up – for Holly's sake more than ours.'

Alan narrowed his eyes. 'Did something happen when you were away?'

Colin took another sip.

'Look, it's none of my business, but, if you want – '

'I met somebody.'

Alan leaned back. 'Thought as much. Are you still in touch?'

Colin shook his head. 'Never even got to first base, to be honest, but I can't get her out of my head.'

'Then you need something to take your mind off it.'

Colin glanced at the plastic bag on the filing cabinet. 'Funny you should say that.'

Alan frowned. 'Why?'

'It's just that I was thinking of taking up a hobby. Maybe a night school class to drag me away from this place.'

'It can't hurt, Col.'

Colin smiled. 'We'll see.'

Chapter Fifty-five

Friday, 2nd May

Colin squinted at the tip of the soldering iron and coaxed the shiny blob to where the resistor terminal poked through the substrate. He dropped the iron into its stand and inspected the finished circuit board. He'd never been interested in electronics, and neat soldering was a skill he'd yet to master, but the end result was better than he'd hoped.

He reached across the desk for the small key, unlocked the drawer and pulled out the modified cycle helmet. He eased the circuit board into the spring clips at the back, and then slid the battery into the plastic holder and pushed the connector into place. He flicked the switch next to the circuit board and smiled when the LED glowed red.

So far, so good ...

He turned the helmet over. The plastic bottle caps hummed softly and tingled his fingers when he touched them.

He clenched his fist. 'Back of the net!'

The front door slammed.

He switched off the helmet and returned it to the drawer.

Jan shouted his name.

Fuck's sake!

Her footsteps sounded on the stairs as he frantically stashed the tools and soldering iron under the desk.

When she entered the study, he was hunched over his laptop.

He looked up and smiled. 'You're back early.'

'Meeting was cancelled,' she said. 'What's your excuse?'

'Alan's stock checking with Kath. I couldn't hear myself think.'

'Can I smell burning?'

He sniffed the air. 'Probably, I think the battery in this laptop's on its last legs.'

She frowned. 'Fancy a brew?'

He grabbed his mug. 'Yeah – ta, Love.'

Chapter Fifty-six

Sunday, 11th May

Colin locked the steel door behind him and made his way to the top floor.

He walked past the kitchen and the room where Eric had died and stopped outside the next door. He pulled the Yale key from his pocket and inserted it into the lock.

Inside, the familiar fusty smell filled his nostrils. He shut the door and surveyed a collection of dusty furniture fifteen years older than him.

He placed the plastic bag on the sofa and removed the helmet. He sat down in the armchair facing the window and placed it on his head. After a couple of minor adjustments, he fastened the chin strap and focussed on the robust, wood-framed television.

His heart was beating faster now.

He took a few deep breaths.

Here we go!

He reached around and flicked the switch at the back of the helmet.

His scalp tingled, and he began to feel sick. The television stayed in focus, but everything else melted into a rotating, blurry kaleidoscope. Within a minute, the effect began to fade, his vision returned to normal and the queasiness subsided.

He glanced around the room. Everything looked the same.

Jesus H! Not again ...

But something *had* changed: there was more natural light now.

He stood up and felt a strange buoyancy in his limbs.

When he glanced at his legs, they were still bent at the knee.

He turned around and saw himself sat in the chair; eyes closed and deathly still like a waxwork dummy.

Fucking hell!

He raised his hand in front of his face, but there was nothing to see. His body was more memory than sensation; a floating breath of consciousness, free of any physical restraints. He laughed, but the sound seemed oddly detached.

He went to the window and gazed out at a very different sky from the one he'd last seen a few minutes ago. Scattered wisps across a wash of grey had turned into columns of swollen white clouds framed in deep azure, and a cluster of unfamiliar smokestacks fed a gloomy pall over the town's northern skyline.

He looked down at the rear yard.

The walls were cleaner and lacked the broken glass, the gates gleamed with bright green paint and a car and motorcycle stood side by side. He couldn't make out the badge on the dark blue bonnet, but the design had to be fifty years old. He recognised the sparkling motorcycle as a Triumph Bonneville.

Across Endell Street, the drab tyre and exhaust centre was now a row of shops with steep roofs and tall chimney stacks.

The pavements bustled with people, but one individual stood out.

He was looking up at the shop.

In fact, he seemed to be staring at Colin.

Is that him?

The man waved, and then glided through the yard wall.

Chapter Fifty-seven

Colin lost sight of him when he passed underneath the fire escape.

A few moments later, a voice spoke his name.

He turned around.

The man was standing at the door, and he wasn't completely solid; a vague impression of the door knob floated in his midriff. He was forty at most, with long hair and dark eyes. The patterned shirt reminded Colin of the one he'd seen on the corpse, and the flared jeans removed any doubt.

'Eric?'

'I see you put my notebooks to good use.'

'This is my third attempt, but I got here in the end.'

He gestured at the armchair. 'It's an improvement on the original.'

'The hard work is all down to you, but a cycle helmet was the obvious choice and saved a lot of time.'

Eric frowned. 'They've changed quite a bit since I was around.'

Colin looked him up and down. 'How come I can see you but not me?'

'Same here,' he said. 'You appear exactly as you do in the chair, minus the helmet.'

'And you're dressed in the clothes you died in.'

'Yeah, I know. For some strange reason, you can see yourself in a mirror.'

'Like a vampire in reverse.'

Eric smiled. 'You could say that – I can only guess it's a mental imprint of how you perceive yourself just before you leave the body. It seems to be projected outward beyond your own frame of reference. You should be able to catch your reflection in the window.'

Colin turned around.

Eric was right, but he was standing in front of a double bed and a large wardrobe.

'I seem to be in another room.'

'It's this room as it was over fifty years ago. Like us, it only shows up as a reflection. The one you're actually in is superimposed on it.'

Colin studied the bizarre juxtaposition, and then turned to Eric. 'No offence, but I thought you'd gone for good.'

'Believe me, I tried, but I couldn't break free from this plane of existence.'

'How so?'

'I really don't know, and it goes against the grain to say it, but I think there might be a purpose to it; a task to fulfil before I can move on.'

'I thought you weren't a religious man.'

'I wasn't, I'm not, not in the traditional sense, but, like I said at Ron's house, there's something beyond here that I can't quite explain.'

'Were you at his grave the other day?'

Eric nodded.

'You scared the shit out of me.'

'Sorry, that wasn't the intention. After I left Josh, I found I could move much more freely. I've shadowed your movements since Ron died, and I know it won't come as a surprise to you when I say it's been something of a roller coaster ride. The graveyard was a half-arsed attempt to make direct contact.'

'And when that failed, you bent the young labourer to your will.'

'I couldn't possess him without the helmet, but I managed to sow a few seeds in his malleable mind. It was the last roll of the dice, but I felt sure you'd want to retrace my steps if you had the notebooks.'

'Mission accomplished,' Colin said. 'And it's been an incredible experience so far, but what's the real reason you've brought me here?'

'To tell you that I'd tracked Wendy from Ambleside all the way to the west coast of Scotland. They took a boat from Mallaig, but I lost them when they rounded Skye.'

'Where were they heading?'

'I couldn't say for sure. Something blocked me from going any further. It was like hitting a brick wall. The last time I experienced anything like it was when I was prevented from returning to my body.'

'What's your best guess?'

'On that bearing, I'd say the Outer Hebrides is a safe bet.'

'If that's the case, they didn't move too far from Thirlmere.'

'Sometimes what you're looking for is right under your nose.'

'Is there anything else you can tell me?'

'The boat was a black, twin-mast ketch called Parmenides. The two men who abducted her were a couple of rough-looking buggers. I didn't get a good look at the crew in Mallaig.'

'The boat's name,' Colin said. 'Is there any significance to it?'

'Maybe … Parmenides is one of the most important pre-Socratic philosophers and the father of metaphysics. He was the first, certainly in Western

Philosophy, to seriously question our perception of reality.'

'Will he give me some insight into what I should do now?'

'Probably not, but I'd start with Mallaig. Hang around there for a while, talk to the locals, eavesdrop their conversations; you're sure to get a lead.'

Colin frowned. 'I'd say that's a long shot.'

'What choice have you got?'

'Maybe I should talk to Anderson.'

'Who?'

'While you were following Wendy north, I was waylaid by a George Smiley character who claimed to be working for the government. He told me Wendy was a human-alien hybrid that the bad guys needed for some undisclosed and nefarious purpose. They let me go because I was of no further use, but I do have a phone number.'

Eric narrowed his eyes. 'Wendy's a hybrid?'

'With psychic abilities.' Colin smiled at the sudden insight. 'She clocked your good self at Ilfracombe harbour.'

'Bloody hell … '

'Apparently, her father used his own sperm to create her. When he found out she was scheduled for dissection, he became disillusioned with the entire project, set fire to the base and smuggled her out.'

'And she never thought to mention any of this?'

'According to Anderson, she knew nothing about it.'

Eric shook his head. 'Do you trust him?'

He shrugged. 'I very much doubt the decision to let me go came solely from the goodness of his heart. They've only just stopped tailing me, which he claimed was for my own protection, but I can't help thinking I'm still on his radar.'

'Then look before you leap. If he's anything like the real Smiley, you need to watch your back.'

'I won't find her on my own, Eric.'

'Could be dangerous to tell him about me.'

'I agree.'

'So what're you going to say when he asks how you know about Mallaig?'

'Christ knows, but I'll have to think of something.'

Eric went to the window. 'How do you like Cranshaw in 1960?'

He joined him. 'This part of town looks better than 2014, to be honest.'

'It does, doesn't it?'

'What're those smokestacks over there?'

'The glass bottle works – Jessops.'

Colin smiled. 'My grandfather worked there.'

'Most of the town worked there, or at Atkins and Sons.'

'My dad used to say progress rarely throws the baby out with the bath water, but the rubber duck ends up in the drain every time.'

'He was right. There's always something lost.'

Colin looked down at the busy shoppers on Endell Street. 'Do you always come back to the same day?'

Eric shook his head. 'Same year, but exactly when seems to be a random event. I've seen every season; morning, noon and night.' He smiled. 'You were lucky to get a nice day.'

They gazed in silence for a while.

'Right then,' Colin said. 'Time I was making tracks.'

'Don't you want to see the old town up close?'

He shook his head. 'Another day perhaps. I've got plenty to do in the present.'

'Best of luck.'

'Thanks, Eric – I'm going to need it.'

'Come here if you want to talk.'

'I'll keep you in the picture.' Colin glanced at his body in the armchair. 'And there is something we need to discuss before I go.'

'At your service.'

'How do I get back into my body?'

'You just have to want to.'

'Go on.'

'Sit back down in the armchair, close your eyes and count to ten.'

Colin opened his eyes and glanced around the room. His neck was stiff, and pins and needles coursed through his fingers and toes. He reached around to flick the switch and took the helmet off. When he stood up, he had to steady himself against the sideboard, but the dizziness soon passed.

At the window, he was relieved to see an empty rear yard and the drab tyre and exhaust centre once again.

When he returned the helmet to the plastic bag, he saw a faint, yellow glow rush across the wall and under the door.

In the corridor, he locked the door and strode towards the front room.

He went to the window and pulled out his phone and the business card with the printed number. He stopped when he tapped the penultimate digit and stared at the screen. Suddenly, this didn't feel like such a good idea.

Look before you leap...

He looked down at the street below.

A taxi pulled out of Endell Street and trundled towards the town centre, leaving a trail of languid black smoke in its wake.

He took a deep breath, tapped the last digit and raised the phone to his ear.

After three metallic clicks and a beep, Anderson answered.

'Good morning, Mr Thurcroft.'

'We need to talk.'

'Are you alone?'

'Yeah, I'm in the shop.'

'You have my undivided attention.'

'I know where she is. Not to a post code, but I can point you in the right direction.'

'Let me stop you there,' Anderson said. 'Is there an open space nearby where we can meet without arousing suspicion?'

'Err … let me think … there's the Municipal Park.'

'That would be ideal. I need you to be there tomorrow at two o'clock.'

'No problem,' Colin said. 'There's an old bandstand not too far from the main gates.'

'I shall see you there,' Anderson said and hung up.

Chapter Fifty-eight

Monday, 12th May

Colin scrunched along the gravel path and glanced at his watch. It was four minutes to two.

A lone figure stood inside the rusty, graffiti spattered bandstand.

Anderson watched impassively as he climbed the wooden stairs, and then greeted him with a brief handshake. 'Good afternoon, Mr Thurcroft.'

'Colin smiled awkwardly. 'Hello again.'

'Tell me what you know.'

He took a deep breath. 'I have it on good authority that Wendy was put on a boat at Mallaig on the west coast of Scotland.'

'What authority?'

'I spoke to another dead man.'

Anderson fixed him with a hard stare.

'It was the most vivid dream I've ever had.'

Anderson sniffed. 'Really, Mr Thurcroft, if you think I've – '

'Eric Manning spoke to me as clearly as I'm speaking to you. He's been trapped between realities since leaving Josh and free to roam at will. He followed her kidnappers until they rounded Skye, where he was stopped from going any further by some unknown presence. He said the boat was a black, twin-mast ketch called Parmenides.'

Anderson surveyed the park.

'I know how mad it sounds, but I wouldn't have phoned you if I wasn't certain.'

'I appreciate what you're saying, but allocating precious time and resources to intelligence gleaned from a dream is somewhat difficult to justify.'

'Maybe I should go up there myself and do some digging.'

Anderson grunted. 'A fool's errand if ever there was one.'

'Have you anything *else* to go on?'

'You should know by now that I can't answer that.'

'She's up there,' Colin said. 'I know it.'

'Have you discussed this with anybody else?'

'Of course not.'

Anderson glanced at his watch. 'Leave it with me.'

'That's it, is it?'

'What did you honestly expect?'

Colin clenched his teeth and shook his head.

Anderson turned to go. 'I shall tell you what I can when I can, but don't hold your breath.'

He watched him to the gates, where a black S60 waited.

When it pulled into the traffic, Colin turned away and chewed his lip.

Across the dead, litter-strewn flower bed, an elderly man watched his Shih Tzu defecate on the grass.

Jan narrowed her eyes. 'Run it past me again?'

Colin topped up his wine. It made lying easier and assuaged the guilt, but he knew too much alcohol could inspire an imaginative deviation from his carefully prepared scenario. So far, the balance was just about right.

He took a quick sip. 'In a nutshell, we set up our outlets in his premises, and he gets fifteen per cent of the takings in lieu of rent.'

'And you met on the internet?'

'LinkedIn.'

'How many shops are we talking about?'

'Err – four – Inverness, Glasgow, Edinburgh and Aberdeen.'

'And they're all empty?'

'Bankrupt businesses bought at knock down prices. He's a real character, a Scottish Delboy, but the market is there, the deal is a good one, and I think I can work with him.'

She sighed. 'When will you be back?'

He took another sip. 'In a week or so.'

'What about the shop?'

'Pete's got it covered. I don't foresee a problem we can't sort out over the phone. If the shit *does* hit the fan, I'll come straight back.'

'And the new government contract?'

'Alan's all over it.'

'If you wait a few weeks, me and Holly could come too.'

'You'd be bored, Jan.'

'In Scotland? Are you kidding?'

'There won't be any sight-seeing detours; I can assure you of that.'

She sighed. 'I'm still surprised you've picked now to do this.'

'It's a great opportunity, and the least I can do is meet him face to face and give the properties a once over.'

'I think you're running before you can walk.'

He shrugged. 'We'll see.'

Chapter Fifty-nine

Wednesday, 14th May

Colin was a few miles north of Gretna when he switched from his docked iPod to Radio Two to catch the Jeremy Vine Show. The midday news had just started.

'More on that earlier report just in. The Scottish port of Mallaig is currently being evacuated due to a problem with a Vanguard class nuclear submarine. All ferry services between Skye and the Western Isles are cancelled and a no fly zone is in place. The Admiralty has stated that the submarine left the Clyde naval base yesterday morning and ran into difficulty shortly after. It's currently resting on the sea bed, and there are no reported casualties, but there is an as yet unconfirmed problem with the reactor which may have leaked radioactive material into the sea. Anyone wanting to enquire about friends and relatives in the area – '

Headlights flashed in the rear view mirror.

He glanced through the steering wheel and saw his speed had dropped below sixty.

He pulled into the middle lane, and the Golf GTi sped past with a snooty glance from the blonde woman in the passenger street.

Normally, he would've responded in kind, but his mind was elsewhere.

Anger and indecision mired the next twenty miles.

The submarine story was plausible, but the evacuation of Mallaig pushed coincidence to breaking point. It was beginning to look as if Anderson had taken him seriously after all. Is that why he'd allowed him to return home? Had he been hoping for a lead like this? Some sort of psychic message from Wendy or Eric? Or was he just a dangling carrot for The Group?'

Bastard! He's played me like a grand piano!

He turned off at Annandale Water Services with the bare bones of a plan.

In the restaurant, he bought a tuna baguette and a large latte and found a table next to a window. He unfurled the map and brought up Google on his phone.

It took less than five minutes to find several suitable companies, but the one closest to the west coast seemed the obvious choice.

He drained his coffee and took the remainder of his baguette back to the car.

He tapped in the phone number and watched a minibus disgorge a company of nuns.

'Good afternoon. Helidonia,' said a woman with a gentle Scottish accent.

'Good afternoon. Would it be possible to charter a flight to the Outer Hebrides this afternoon?'

'Whereabouts exactly?'

'Wherever's best for you, to be honest.'

'There's a temporary no fly zone in that area, sir.'

'Yeah, I've just heard.' He consulted the map. 'Okay … let's see … can you get me as close to the northerly limit as possible?'

'Bear with me a moment.'

He heard muffled voices.

'We could take you to Tarbert if you arrive before three o'clock.'

He ran his finger across the map. 'What would it cost?'

'One way?'

'Err … yeah. For now anyway.'

More muffled voices.

'You'd be looking at eight hundred pounds plus VAT.'

Colin winced. 'That's fine. I'm on my way.'

'What name is it?'

'Thurcroft – Colin Thurcroft.'

'We'll need some form of identity when you arrive.'

'Driver's licence?'

'That will be fine. See you soon, Mr Thurcroft.'

'Bye.'

He folded the map away and bit into the baguette.

Eight hundred plus VAT! That's going to take some explaining ...

The minibus driver locked the door and lit a cigarette.

Chapter Sixty

He arrived at the small airfield a little before two and followed the hand-painted sign to Helidonia. He parked the car next to a battered Land Rover and walked towards the portacabin. Inside, a pale young woman with long auburn hair sat behind a small counter.

She closed her paperback and smiled warmly. 'Mr Thurcroft?'

'It is,' he said.

'I'm Rhona Hamilton. Dad's just gone to refuel – he shouldn't be long.'

He pulled out his wallet and offered his credit card and driver's licence.

She glanced at the licence and slipped his card into the reader. 'That's nine hundred and sixty pounds exactly.'

He tapped in his PIN number. 'I'll need picking up in a day or two – I *might* have somebody with me, but I can't be more specific at the moment.'

'No problem at all. Just give us a call when you're ready.'

'Is it okay to leave my car here?'

'That's fine.' She offered the receipt and card. 'But it's at your own risk, and we'll need a set of keys.'

Colin put his car keys on the counter. 'Thanks.'

'Would you like something to drink while you wait?'

'White coffee, one sugar would be great, thanks.'

'Coming up,' she said and slipped through the door behind her.

He sat down on a plastic chair and lifted the Daily Express from the low table. He skimmed through it, but there was no mention of the stricken submarine.

She returned with the coffee and placed it on the table.

'Thanks,' he said and took a sip.

She gestured at his rucksack. 'Where're you planning to walk?'

'I had intended to drive to Skye and get the ferry from Uig to Lochmaddy to meet up with some friends. The problem with the nuclear sub means we'll have to convene at Tarbert and find some routes around Lewis.'

Word perfect!

'You won't be disappointed,' she said. 'If the weather holds, that is.'

'That's good to know.'

She returned to her book and Colin to the newspaper.

A few minutes later, the noise of rotor blades grew steadily louder. It called to mind a dark helicopter hovering over tall conifers, and he swallowed hard when the unpleasant memories flooded back.

Rhona went to the window. 'Here he is now.'

He joined her and watched a gleaming white helicopter land on the concrete strip. He recognised the clever logo from the website: a Saint Andrew's Cross rotor on a boldly stylised fuselage.

'It's his new toy,' she said. 'He's wanted a twin-engine for some time.'

'How many do you operate?'

'Two – my brother took the 206 to Edinburgh to chauffeur a property bigwig and his entourage.' She smiled. 'Dad thinks he's a gangster, but he pays well.'

The pilot turned towards them and gave the thumbs up.

Rhona returned the gesture. 'He's ready for you now, Mr Thurcroft.'

Colin leaned into the wash from the rotor and jogged towards the open passenger door. The pilot was a solidly built man of around fifty with curly ginger hair and a greying beard. He wore dark glasses and a faded blue jumpsuit.

He leaned across and shook Colin's hand. 'Kit Hamilton. Nice tae meet ye.'

'And you,' Colin said.

'Dae ye wanna sit in the front or back?'

'Front, if that's okay.'

'Nae bother. Hoy yer rucksack in the back.'

Colin did as instructed, and then climbed in and shut the door. With a little help from Kit, he strapped himself into the harness and put on the headset.

'Kin ye hear me okay?' Kit said.

'Loud and clear.'

Kit quickly ran through the emergency procedures.

'Any questions?'

Colin shook his head. 'I don't think so.'

'Arrway we go then.'

His stomach lightened as they rose and rotated.

They climbed steadily for a few minutes before Kit spoke again.

'Have ye travelled by helicopter afore, Mr Thurcroft?'

'No – this is my first time.'

'Ah'm gaun tae stay at aroon eight hundred feet o'er land, sae ye can take in the scenery, but we'll have tae go tae two thousand when we reach the sea.'

'Okay,' Colin said. 'How long before we get there?'

'Aboot an hour – maybe a wee bit longer.'

For the next twenty minutes, Kit punctuated the flight with comments on the beautiful west highland scenery, pointing out natural features here and there.

When the shoreline came into view his tone cooled a little. 'Mind if I ask why ye want tae go tae Tarbert?'

Colin recounted the same hiking story he'd related to Rhona.

Kit made no comment, and they flew in silence for a while.

'If ye in a bit o' a situation, ah might be able tae help.'

'Sorry?'

'Yer hiking story doesnae ring true.'

Colin felt a flush of heat on his neck. 'And why's that?'

'Ye phoned the office wioot a specific destination, but then ye shell oot the best part o' a grand tae get as close as possible tae a nae fly zone o'er a damaged sub.'

This is all I need!

'Ye meet all sorts ay folk in this job, and ah've been doing it fir o'er thaety years. Ah'm a law-abiding fella maysel, but ah've learned tae turn a blind eye wi some ay ma more colourful clients.'

Colin frowned. 'Am I colourful?'

A broad smile creased Kit's face. 'Nah, but ah ken you've git somethin mair important on yer mind than meeting up wi hiking pals.'

'Like what?'

Kit shrugged. 'A wee story fir a newspaper perhaps.'

'I'm not a journalist – I sell hiking gear.'

Kit's frankness had taken him off-guard, but he seemed genuine, and his offer of help was tempting.

Sod it! What have I got to lose?

264

'I'm looking for somebody,' Colin said flatly.

Kit glanced at him but said nothing.

'All I know is she's somewhere in the Outer Hebrides – I'm pretty sure she's still alive, but I don't know how long that'll last.'

'Are the polis involved?'

Colin shook his head. 'I wish they were. Unfortunately, it's not an option, even though she's done nothing wrong and neither have I.'

'Noo ah'm intrigued.'

'I've said too much.'

'The offer ay help is still on the table.'

'Let's hear it then.'

'In case ye hadnae noticed, the Ooter Hebrides is an island chain, stretching fir o'er a hundred miles. It's largely uninhabited, there's nae but a handful ay roads, and the coastline is treacherous tae the unwary.'

'You don't fancy my chances then.'

'Put the military intae the mix, and ah'd say they're close tae zero.'

'So how can *you* help?'

'Ah canna, but ah ken a man who can. He's a larger than life character who's arwais up fir an adventure on the high seas. He lives ten miles or so up the coast from Tarbert, but he runs a boat oot o' there.'

'I didn't intend to get anybody else involved.'

'Yerl get naewhere wioot somebodie who kens the isles like he does.'

Colin frowned. 'Can you get in touch with him?'

Kit pulled a phone from his pocket and tapped the screen. 'Nae bother at all.' He slipped the headset around his neck and put the phone to his ear.

'Maurie, ye auld bastard. How are ye?' He threw his head back and laughed. 'How did yae ken it wis me?'

He laughed again. 'Listen up, ah'm wi a customer who could dae wi yer help.' He glanced at Colin and winked. 'Missing person, Maurie, somewhere in The Isles, and he doesnae want the boys in blue involved – aye, ah wid say so – he's a Sassenach like yersel – aye – aye, okay – aboot forty minutes or so – see ye soon, pal. Have the kettle on.' He hung up and slipped the phone into his pocket.

Colin waited for him to adjust the headset. 'What happens now?'

'Ye have tae convince him his time is nae better spent.'

They were over Skye now, and Kit hugged the barren, jagged peaks and plunging valleys with consummate skill. Colin had heard descriptions of this island from hikers and seen countless photographs and internet images, but none of them had done it justice. It was absolutely breath-taking.

When towering, primordial rock gave way to rolling green hills, they veered north and followed a shoreline of steep cliffs and crashing waves.

Twenty minutes later, they reached the open sea and started to climb.

As they levelled out, Kit nudged him and pointed at something over to the south.

Colin shielded his eyes and saw a long grey slab on the glittering water.

'Royal Navy,' Kit said. 'Looks like a destroyer tae me.'

The spectacular scenery had taken Colin's mind off the task ahead, but the warship was an unsettling wake up call.

'Tell me about Maurie,' he said.

'Christ Almighty! Where dae ah start? He wis somethin ay a mover and shaker in the acid hoose scene in the earlie nineties. He ran a couple o' clubs in Ibiza and Majorca but got oot when things started tae git heavy. He's a borderline recluse, but ah dae occasionally fly o'er some well-heeled types and lassies young enough tae be his bairns.'

'How old is he?'

'Earlie sixties, but he keeps hissel pretty trim.'

'And he likes getting out on the water?'

'Oh aye. He's a regular Jack bloody Sparrow in that auld cabin cruiser.'

A long, thin strip of dark grey stretched across the horizon.

They flew in silence again, and Colin began to make out mountains and hills over swathes of olive green.

As they neared, he saw a red and white lighthouse at the mouth of a wide bay.

Kit followed the rocky shoreline to the small harbour town of Tarbert, and on to where the Isle of Harris met the North Atlantic. He descended over the spume-flecked waves and turned inland, across a sandy beach, to a whitewashed, single-storey cottage. He circled over it, scattering grey smoke from the squat chimney, and landed in a field about thirty yards from the rear yard.

A man left the back door and strode towards them.

He was tall and tanned with grey hair tied back in a ponytail. A red Tibetan shirt and baggy brown shorts fluttered in the dying rotor wash. When he reached the helicopter, his broad smile flashed a gold incisor and deepened the wrinkles under vivid blue eyes.

He shook Kit's hand and slapped him on the shoulder. 'Christopher Hamilton, you big ginger tosser!'

His accent was Estuary English.

Kit laughed. 'Maurice Corner, ye auld letch. Yer lookin well.'

'Hanging in there, old boy.'

Colin leaned across and shook his hand. 'Colin Thurcroft. Nice to meet you.'

'And you, mate,' he said. 'You're very welcome.'

Maurie took Colin to the cottage, leaving Kit to secure the helicopter.

The aroma of burning wood suffused the low beamed kitchen. Flaccid socks and gaudy boxer shorts drooped from a drying rack suspended over a sooty aga, and a wide Belfast sink teemed with dirty pans and dishes.

He gestured at the long oak table. 'Park your arse, Colin. I'll make the Rosy.'

Colin placed his rucksack on the stone floor and sat down on a lath back chair. 'Thanks for agreeing to see me. I really appreciate it.'

'No worries. I like the solitary life, but it's nice to have company once in a while.'

'How long have you lived here?'

'Ten years, give or take.' He emptied the kettle into three mugs. 'Best thing I ever did, mate – I'll end my days up here.'

'How did you meet Kit?'

'Same as you, I guess; I needed a helicopter in a hurry.'

'He said you'd be up for a nautical adventure.'

Maurie placed the mugs on the table and winked. 'We'll get the big yin out of the way, and then you can give me the lowdown.' He went to the fridge freezer and took out a carton of milk. 'Whatever the outcome, you're welcome to stay the night.'

'Thanks, that's very kind of you.'

Kit entered and took a seat opposite.

Colin sipped his tea and listened with growing amusement as Kit and Maurie exchanged gossip about mutual friends and acquaintances. Some of the ribald tales made him realise just how tame his own social life was.

Fifteen minutes later, Kit drained his mug and announced his departure.

He hugged Maurie, and then shook hands with Colin and wished him good luck.

They went outside to wave him off.

When the helicopter reached the sea, Maurie turned to Colin. 'Fancy a *proper* drink?'

'Go on then,' he said. 'You've twisted my arm.'

Chapter Sixty-one

Maurie led him through the kitchen, into a spacious lounge.

A tired, cream leather suite faced a vast TV screen on a chimney breast stacked with gnarled logs. Framed gold disks dotted the rough plaster walls. Four tall cabinets, crammed with LPs and CDs, loomed over top-quality hi-fi separates in a steel rack.

Maurie went over to a dark wood bureau piled with spirit bottles and glass tumblers and poured two generous measures of Jura single malt. 'How do you take it, Colin?'

'As it comes, thanks.'

He handed him a glass and gestured at the sofa. 'Park your arse, amigo.'

Colin did as instructed and took a sip.

Maurie sat down in an armchair and lifted a square glass plate from the hearth. Colin watched transfixed as he took a short straw and proceeded to snort a thin line of white powder into each nostril.

He blinked furiously and offered the plate to him.

'No thanks.' he said and raised his glass. 'I'll stick with this.'

Maurie returned the plate to the hearth. 'Kit said you're looking for somebody.'

'That's right.'

'Okay, let's hear it.'

'There's a lot I can't tell you.'

'How come?'

'I can't even divulge that, to be honest.'

'That's not how it works, mate.' Maurie leaned forward and fixed him with dilated pupils. 'I need more than that before I put my scrawny neck on the line.'

Colin held his gaze, but the sudden mood swing was disconcerting.

Is that the coke talking?

'Believe me, it's best you don't know.'

'Let me be the judge of that.'

'If you won't help, I'll have to go it alone.'

Maurie grunted. 'And how far do you think you'll get?'

'I don't know, but I'm going to have to try.'

Maurie sighed. 'Okay, tell me what you can.'

'This nuclear sub problem – it's a smokescreen.'

'For what exactly?'

'I very much doubt you'd believe me if I told you.'

'Try me.'

Colin ran his fingers through his hair.

'Come on, mate,' Maurie said. 'At least whet my appetite.'

He's right. I need to give him something.

'My friend got mixed up in a fracas between our secret services and a renegade group of scientists. She was taken by force to a secret base somewhere in these islands. The stricken sub story is hiding a concerted effort to find her and shut down the base.'

Maurie snorted. 'No fuckin' way!'

'Yes fucking way, Maurie, but I wouldn't blame you if you thought I'd lost the plot.'

Maurie frowned and studied him. 'Christ on a bike. You're serious, aren't you?'

Colin nodded. 'Yes, I am – deadly serious.'

'What a complete clusterfuck.'

Colin flashed a wry smile. 'Not a bad summary.'

Maurie sipped his whisky. 'What goes on at this base?'

'I can't go into that.'

'Quelle surprise!'

'Sorry … '

'And you think *we* can locate this place *before* the secret services?'

'Goes without saying it's somewhere within the no-fly zone, and I've good reason to believe it's close to the coast. If you can get me to North Uist, without attracting unwelcome attention, I'll take it from there.'

'And what do you intend to do if you find it?'

'To be honest, I'm still working on that.'

Maurie rolled his eyes.

'I don't expect you to put your neck on the line, Maurie. If you think it's too risky, I'll understand.'

'Let me think about it.'

They sipped their whiskies in silence for a while.

Colin shuffled in his seat. 'Can I ask *you* a question?'

'Fill your boots.'

'Have you ever come across a twin-mast ketch called Parmenides?'

'Too right I have! Bastard thing almost ran into me about a year ago! It runs supplies to a monastery on North Uist. I say monastery, but I've never seen anybody in a habit claiming to herald from there.'

Colin's heart missed a beat. 'That's where she is!'

'In a monastery?'

'She was put aboard that ketch at Mallaig a month ago.'

'How do you know that?'

'Doesn't matter,' Colin said. 'What do you know about this *so-called* monastery?'

'Just that it was built around a ruined church not long after I moved up here.'

'Will you take me to it?'

Maurie frowned. 'I've done some mad things in my time.'

'Is that a *yes* or a *no*?'

'If I have any doubts, I'll turn us around and head straight back to Tarbert.'

'Fair enough.'

'Not sure how you'll get up there; it's perched on the edge of a fuckin' cliff.'

'I'll face that problem nearer the time. How soon can we sail?'

'Hold on, and I'll check.'

Maurie got up and went into the kitchen.

Colin leaned back and drained his glass. He gasped as the whisky burned its way down to his stomach.

A few moments later, Maurie returned to his seat with a laptop. 'Weather looks okay tomorrow.' He tapped the keypad. 'And high tide's late-morning, so we can go around noon.'

'How long will it take?'

'At cruising speed, we'll be there in three hours tops, which gives me enough time to get back before dark.'

'That's great,' Colin said. 'And I insist on paying you for your trouble.'

'That won't be necessary.'

'At least let me – '

Maurie raised his hand. 'Seriously, it's not a problem.'

'I can't thank you enough.'

'No worries, mate.' He gestured at Colin's empty glass. 'And you can bless the venture by helping yourself to another dram.'

Colin stood up. 'Cheers, I think I will. Can I get *you* one?'

Maurie shook his head and threw his legs over the arm of the chair. 'You never know, we might even meet the Uist Shoney.'

Colin poured another generous measure of Jura. 'The what?'

'If you spend any length of time in these isles, you'll hear stories about sea serpents and kelpies and other wee beasties, but the Uist Shoney is a new creature, or maybe a reinvented one. I can't quite decide myself.'

He sat down. 'Go on.'

'It all kicked off with a story on the local news. Apparently, a couple of kids found something unusual washed up on a beach near Hosta. They went off to tell their parents, but, when they returned, it'd gone. It was described as a very large octopus, off-white in colour, with one big compound eye like an insect's. Since then, there've been a couple of sightings of similar creatures out at sea which were said to be glowing.'

He sipped his whisky. 'How long ago was this?'

'The beach story goes back about three years, and I haven't heard about anything at sea since last summer.'

'What's your take on it?'

Maurie shrugged. 'The kids found a dead, bloated octopus that got washed back into the sea before their parents got there. The offshore sightings could be anything with bioluminescence; squid being the obvious culprits in this case.'

He nodded. 'You're probably right.'

The conversation wandered, in turn, to Maurie's eventful past and Colin's family and business. After the third glass of malt, Maurie's eyes began to close.

Colin continued to talk until he heard him snore, and then got up and left the cottage.

He found a path behind the garage and walked down to a beach bordered by low dunes crowned with clumps of long, windswept grass. The briny Atlantic breeze and the cries of gulls went some way to sober him up as he strolled along the smooth sand.

After about half a mile, the beach curved out to a headland of large, angular rocks.

He climbed to the top and sat down on a wide ledge.

The glinting sea stretched to a horizon tinged by the first blush of evening.

He stayed there for the best part of an hour, lost in the events of the last few weeks, and watched the sun sink through the ruddy clouds. With the light fading fast, he climbed down and made his way back to the cottage.

It was dark when he entered the lounge and found Maurie still asleep.

That night, Maurie cooked frozen lasagne and oven chips. After several more whiskies and some hit and miss channel surfing, Colin made his excuses and retired to the spare room. He phoned Jan, who sussed he'd had one too many, and told her he was in Glasgow.

A little after midnight, he fell asleep to The Lark Ascending on his iPod.

Chapter Sixty-two

Maurie clamped the slice of toast between his teeth and lifted the creaky garage door. Inside, a vintage, metallic-green Porsche 911 gleamed in the late morning sun.

He turned to Colin. 'A 1976 Carrera 3 – best of the breed, in my opinion.'

'I wouldn't know,' Colin said. 'But I'll take your word for it.'

Maurie took a last bite and tossed the crust into a clump of nettles. He wiped his hands on his jeans and pulled out a set of car keys. 'Lock up for me, will you?'

Colin gave him the thumbs up.

Maurie sidled into the garage, and, a few moments later, the flat-six engine rumbled into life, and the car rolled forward. Colin dropped the door and closed the lock. He took a few deep breaths of sea air and gazed, with sudden trepidation, at the limitless expanse of slate-grey ocean. When Maurie sounded the horn, he picked up his rucksack and strode towards the car.

Maurie trundled up a bumpy track and turned onto a narrow road, where he accelerated with stomach-churning haste and an angry growl from the exhaust. He clearly relished driving fast along the winding tarmac, and Colin found himself gripping the seat a little too often for comfort.

They reached Tarbert in less than fifteen minutes and parked next to the Tourist Information Centre. They strolled past the deserted ferry terminal and met a friend of Maurie's, who he introduced as "Andy". He was about the same age as Maurie with thick grey hair and a close beard. Colin had struggled at times to understand

Kit Hamilton, but Andy's accent was almost unintelligible.

He rowed them out to a cabin cruiser moored about sixty yards from the slipway.

As they approached, Colin surveyed what was undoubtedly an old but well-cared for boat. It was about twenty-five feet in length and eight wide. The dark green hull looked freshly painted and the wooden cabin gleamed with thick varnish. A black canvas awning covered most of the rear deck. On the bow, he read the name *Candice* in white serif capitals.

They thanked Andy and climbed aboard.

Colin helped Maurie to dismantle the awning and stow it away.

After a quick guided tour of the galley, Maurie went to winch up the anchor, and Colin made tea and coffee. As he poured the milk, he heard the engine start, and a brief vibration ran through the floor. He took the drinks up to the helm and got comfortable on the padded seat across from Maurie.

The engine revs increased, and the boat moved off.

'How do you like her?' Maurie said.

'She's a bonnie boat, Captain Corner, and that's for sure.'

Maurie laughed. 'She is that.'

'Did you name her Candice?'

The humour fled from Maurie's face. 'I did … '

'If I'm prying, Maurie, just tell – '

'You're not, mate. It was a long time ago, but the wound's still raw.'

Colin sipped his coffee.

'Candice was a wild child who flew too close to the sun. I blamed some serious players for her death, and they didn't like it, so I cashed in my chips and got the fuck out.'

'Sorry to hear that.'

Maurie shrugged. 'It was great while it lasted, when it was just a few mad bastards out for a good time – 'til everybody and his fuckin' dog wanted in on it.'

Colin changed the subject to technical questions about the boat.

The going was smooth until they reached the lighthouse and the open sea. Here, the waves steepened, and the boat began to heave and sway.

Colin fought the queasiness, but it was a losing battle.

'All right, Colin?' Maurie said. 'Looking a bit green round the gills, mate.'

It was all that was needed to make him rush to the stern and puke his coffee and breakfast into The Minch. He returned to his seat, but, less than a minute later, he was back at the stern dry retching. He couldn't remember ever feeling this rough; it was like the worst car sickness mixed with the mother of all hangovers.

On Maurie's advice, he went below and found some bright blue pills in the medical cabinet. He washed a couple down with a glass of water and lay on the small bed at the front of the cabin and tried not to look through the port holes.

The gentle creak of timber, the muted drone from the engine and the slap of waves on the hull combined into a soothing lullaby.

He closed his eyes and turned onto his side.

He woke suddenly and saw Maurie standing over him.

'How you feeling, mate?'

Colin sat up and rubbed his eyes. 'My heads a bit muzzy and my mouth feels like sandpaper. Apart from that, not too bad.'

Maurie offered a glass of water. 'Here, drink this and get your arse on deck.'

'How long have I been out?'

Maurie turned to go. 'Put it this way, we're almost there.'

He drained the glass and got to his feet.

The boat wasn't moving around as much now, but his legs felt wobbly, and he had to steady himself on the fixtures and fittings to reach the deck.

He took a couple of deep breaths of sea air, and his head started to clear.

Over to port, about a mile away, a dark cliff rose at least fifty feet above the breakers. A group of grey buildings and a square bell tower clung to its flat summit.

He pointed in that direction. 'Is that it?'

Maurie nodded. 'There's a beach not too far away, but I'd run aground before I could get you near enough. According to the charts, the best bet is a flat rock ledge, about fifty yards out.'

'Whatever you think's best, Maurie – I'm in your hands.' Colin surveyed the cliff. 'Where do you think the Parmenides loads and unloads?'

'Hard to say,' Maurie said. 'They could anchor offshore and bring stuff in by boat – I've only ever seen it at sea.'

A few minutes later, Colin saw a swathe of glistening rock and seaweed jutting through the waves. He went below to fetch his rucksack.

Maurie turned to starboard and brought Candice alongside.

Colin fastened the chest and waist straps tight. 'Thanks again, Maurie. You're an absolute star.'

Maurie smiled warmly. 'You're not so bad yourself, mate. Now fuck off before my boat gets smashed to matchwood.'

'Aye, aye, Captain.'

'Best of luck,' Maurie said. 'I hope you find her.'

Colin stepped gingerly onto the gunwale and gripped the cabin roof. His legs still felt a bit like somebody else's, but there was no going back now.

He waited for the swell to take him above the rock.

Jesus H! This is hairy!

When it did, he hesitated and missed his chance.

Come on! Come on!

As it rose again, he leapt across and slipped on a clump of seaweed, landing on his rucksack like an upturned beetle.

Maurie laughed. 'Mind how you go on the green stuff!'

Colin grinned and struggled to his feet. 'Thanks for the warning!'

They waved as the boat pulled away and headed out to sea.

He began to pick his way over the rocks. He fought for balance on every one and was relieved to reach the beach and feel soft sand under his boots.

He turned towards the open sea.

Maurie was some distance away now, but he wasn't alone.

A smaller, much faster craft was approaching Candice from the south.

Chapter Sixty-three

Colin wriggled out of his rucksack and rummaged inside for the compact binoculars. He crouched down and stared through them into pitch black.

Fuck's sake!

He tore off the lens cap and brought the boats into focus.

The motorised dinghy drew alongside, and three men, in dark jumpsuits and helmets, stood up and pointed assault rifles. Maurie raised his hands, and two of the men jump on-board. Colin lost sight of them when they move into the cabin.

His heart pounded, and the binoculars trembled in his hands.

After what seemed like an age, one of the men returned to the dinghy.

The smaller craft sped away and headed back south.

A few moments later, Candice followed at a slower pace. As the boat turned, he saw Maurie at the wheel with one of the men stood behind him.

When they disappeared around the headland, Colin got to his feet and trudged across the beach to a hollow in the side of the cliff. Inside, he sat down on a large boulder and ran his fingers through his hair.

What have I done?

The armed men could be protecting the base or actively trying to get inside. Either way, it was immaterial as he was in danger from both sides now. He felt sure they hadn't seen him, but it was only a matter of time before Maurie blabbed. If he hadn't already. And who could blame him? And what about

Maurie? How would they make him talk? And what would happen to him afterwards?

What the fuck have I done?

He mulled the situation over for several minutes in a forlorn attempt to assuage some of the crushing guilt, but it was no good. Albeit unintentionally, he'd dropped an innocent man well and truly in the shit, and there was nothing he could do about it.

Except do what I came here to do ...

The insight brought him back to the task in hand.

He returned the binoculars to the rucksack and surveyed his surroundings. What he'd assumed to be little more than a shallow depression in the cliff face was actually a dark, voluminous cave. At the back, a patch of rock glistened in a shaft of weak sunlight.

But something less obvious had grabbed his attention.

Over to the right, there was just enough light to make out steep, roughly-hewn steps, winding up into the rock. He went across and made a cautious ascent to a heavy, rust-streaked door without a handle. He ran his fingers around the edge, but there was nothing to grip on to. He thought about banging it with his fists but quickly changed his mind.

There must be another way in ...

He descended the steps and went over to the shaft of sunlight. He clamped the rucksack to his chest and climbed through the fissure, into a narrow crevasse.

The almost vertical walls reached a good thirty feet from the smooth sand floor to a jagged strip of ashen sky. A pungent, briny tang filled his nostrils.

He followed it for a good fifty yards to a rock ledge perched twenty feet above the furthest inland extent of a wide, sandy bay enclosed by grassy hills and peppered with dark boulders and glinting rock pools framed in clumps of limp seaweed. Only the distant cry of gulls carried on the gentle breeze.

He crouched down and reached into the rucksack for his binoculars.

Along the shoreline, some three hundred yards away, two empty landing craft rested with their ramps open. Over to the right, a swathe of thick ropes dangled from a sheer cliff face at least forty feet in height. He could just make out the dark roofs of a couple of long, single-storey buildings. He'd arrived too late to witness the start of the attack, but it was obviously still in progress.

He adjusted the focus wheel and scanned the grey silhouette on the overcast horizon. He knew little of modern warships, but the sparse, angular contours left little doubt that it was one of the new Type Forty-something destroyers discussed on a recent current affairs TV programme.

The sound of a muffled explosion reached him from the direction of the cliff.

He turned towards it and adjusted the focus wheel again.

A ball of grey smoke rose from one of the buildings and dissolved into the breeze. Bursts of automatic gunfire preceded another slightly louder explosion.

Something sparkled briefly in the corner of his left eye.

He panned the binoculars across the sand until he saw it again at the side of one of the largest and nearest boulders. At first, he thought it was coming from a rock pool, but then it moved up and behind the boulder.

His heartbeat quickened as he studied the ancient contours.

There it was again, but on the other side.

It flashed again and faded to reveal the twin lenses of another pair of binoculars held by a figure in dark clothing.

Jesus H!

He backed into the crevasse and brought the boulder into view again.

There was nothing there now.

A noise from behind spun him around.

A flurry of dry sand and small stones tumbled into the crevasse.

He stared up at the towering rock walls.

What the ...?

High above, on the opposite side, a pale object slipped from sight.

It was only a glimpse, but Colin retained a clear mental image of something resembling a large, water-filled balloon.

It purged the man with the binoculars clean from his thoughts.

He stood up and put on his rucksack without taking his eyes from the spot, but it didn't reappear.

He edged along the crevasse, scanning each side in turn.

About ten feet ahead, more stones rattled down onto the sand.

He stopped and searched the steep rock in vain.

He moved forward again with his hand over his eyes, straining to catch the slightest movement from above.

He didn't notice Wendy until he almost bumped into her.

Chapter Sixty-four

Colin reeled back and steadied himself against the rock.

As far as he could tell, she looked exactly like she had in the nightmare.

A limp, surgical gown hung from her hunched shoulders and several electrodes still clung to her shaved head. The serene smile was unsettling, but her eyes held his with their familiar vitality.

Colin turned his attention to her companion.

He was quite tall, probably in his late fifties or early sixties, with unruly greying hair. His eyes were little more than slits under a deeply-line forehead, and a trickle of dried blood ran from his left nostril to a humourless, thin-lipped mouth framed by a square jaw. He wore a crumpled white shirt rolled up to the elbows and grey trousers streaked with dirt.

Colin didn't realise he had a gun until he pointed it at him.

'I've no idea who you are,' he said. 'But you need to get out of my way.'

His accent was mid-Atlantic, and he sounded like he meant it.

Colin turned to Wendy.

Her lips didn't move but he heard her voice.

Colin?

It was in his head.

Wendy?

His question was too.

Yes, it's me. He can't hear us, but you need to do as he says.

Colin replied: *I can't just stand aside and let him take you.*

285

He'll shoot you if you don't!

'I said move,' the man said.

Do as he says, Colin.

Colin held his ground, but his will was crumbling.

He organised the coup at Thirlmere. Don't call his bluff.

'This is your last chance!' the man said through gritted teeth.

Colin stepped aside, but the man didn't move.

His gaze was fixed on something directly ahead of him, and his gun followed suit.

Colin turned around and saw three men approaching from the end of the crevasse.

They were dressed in black combat gear and bullet proof vests. The smaller, unarmed man in the middle wore spectacles and a dark beanie; and looked oddly familiar. The other two wore helmets with tinted visors and carried compact assault rifles close to their chests.

They stopped ten feet away, and Colin recognised the unarmed man as Anderson.

'Good Afternoon, Mr Thurcroft,' he said. 'I trust you are in fine fettle.'

'Fucking brilliant,' Colin said blankly.

Anderson turned to the man. 'And you, Alex?'

'Oh, I'm absolutely spiffing, old boy,' the man replied with undisguised sarcasm.

'Excellent. Now, how about you put the gun down, and we sort this mess out?'

'How about I shoot you straight through your supercilious face?'

Anderson flashed a cold smile. 'The man before us, Mr Thurcroft, is Professor Alex Jeprell. A scientist of similar abilities to Ms Cooper's late father, but without a scrap of his decency or empathy.'

Jeprell sneered. 'Hardly qualities you possess.'

Anderson took a step forward. 'Do not confuse my determination to thwart your plans with the complete absence of a conscience, Jeprell.'

Jeprell nuzzled the barrel into Wendy's temple. 'Then this is where you achieve your altruistic goal.'

The soldiers aimed their rifles at Jeprell.

Anderson raised his hand. 'Let's not get carried away now, Alex.'

Wendy seemed oblivious. She breathed deeply and closed her eyes.

Several small stones tumbled down from above.

Everybody scanned the top of the crevasse.

They're here, Colin.

Who?

Lyrans.

What? I thought they'd left.

They did, but the Thirlmere hybrids were unstable. The Lyran genes replicated and absorbed the human components. They escaped from here years ago, but they made telepathic contact with me shortly after I arrived.

What do they want?

Me.

'Expecting company?' Anderson said.

Jeprell glared at Anderson, but the arrogance had gone.

More stones tumbled onto the sand, but this time they came from both sides of the crevasse.

A wave of pale, bulbous forms on countless sinuous limbs hurried down the crevasse walls.

Jeprell and the soldiers aimed wildly, but they didn't get chance to fire. The weapons leapt from their grasps

287

when Wendy raised her arms. They hung ten feet in the air, spinning slowly.

The creatures continued their descent.

Three of them reached out their limbs, the ends of which morphed into primitive hands, and plucked the weapons from the air. They wrapped them tight, and the sound of snapping metal reverberated around the crevasse. The smashed rifles and handgun dropped to the sand.

Jeprell slumped down and bowed his head.

The two soldiers back away, but Anderson stood his ground.

At least a dozen Lyrans now filled the crevasse behind Wendy. Their pallid, translucent bodies were octopus-like. Squatting on six arched legs, they stood a good five feet tall. A large, multi-faceted eye dominated the smooth oblong head, but it wasn't the insect structure Maurie had described; concentric, overlapping rings of variously shaped, iridescent segments radiated out from a small black pupil. There were no other features he could see; nothing to suggest a mouth, nose or ears.

Wendy lowered her arms. She took a few steps towards Anderson and spoke out loud for the first time.

'What happens next can't be stopped, but you can prevent further bloodshed if you get the forces under your command to keep their distance.'

'And what does happen next?'

'The final phase.'

'Which is?'

'The rescue and cultivation of human civilisation.'

Anderson opened his mouth but no words formed.

Wendy glared at him. 'Now do as I say and call off the attack dogs.'

288

He pulled a small walkie-talkie from a pouch on his chest. His hand was shaking as he raised it to his mouth. 'Zero Eight to Sabre One.'

The crackly reply came almost immediately. 'Come in, Zero Eight. Over.'

'Report status. Over.'

'Base secure. Over.'

'Roger, Sabre One. Stand down and remain in position. Over.'

'Wilco. Out.'

He returned the walkie-talkie and met Wendy's gaze. 'In their kennels.'

She turned to Colin. 'Are you okay?'

He mustered an uncertain smile and nodded.

She looked into his eyes, and he heard her voice in his head again.

Everything will be okay, Colin. Trust me.

She turned to Anderson. 'The soldiers are to stay here with the professor. You must come with us.'

Jeprell looked up at Anderson with an expression that was hard to read.

Anderson turned to the soldiers. 'Do as she says.'

Chapter Sixty-five

The Lyrans led the way along the crevasse, and into the cave. When they reached the beach, they fanned out in a rough semi-circle around the three of them.

Wendy turned to Anderson.

'Jeprell wanted to reshape humanity to his blueprint and eradicate the inferior.' She gave him a wry smile. 'The aim of the people you strive for was not so different.'

'We meant no harm,' Anderson said. 'With you, we could improve the human genome in so many ways: eradicate disease, raise intelligence, prolong life – '

'But harm always results from such meddling. The Lyrans recreated themselves from the ground up, but only when they'd reached a far more advanced stage of cerebral evolution. Compared to them, you're children playing with a chemistry set that's missing its instructions. Whatever the intention, an elitist hegemony or a brutal dystopia was just around the corner. Take your pick.'

'And how is your *final phase* so different?'

'The difference is measured improvement rather than ham-fisted upgrade.'

'Tell me more.'

'Not in your lifetime, but the hour will come when this planet must be wrested from human control. The crash in 1951 wasn't the first time beings from the Lyra star cluster have visited this planet, albeit in a more controlled manner. Others, from many far flung systems, come here for largely opportunistic reasons, but the Lyrans adopted a more benevolent approach and, in consequence, a radical agenda. Intervention was first discussed over a hundred years ago, and the final decision was made before the third sphere hit Siberia.'

'Based on what?'

'I'm surprised you ask. The reasons have been plain to see for many years, and the tipping point is fast approaching.'

'How will this be implemented?'

'That I can't say, but it will be done without bloodshed and with more compassion than you might expect. The human race will be given the time and resources to grow and develop, but under the guidance and jurisdiction of a superior species unencumbered by the greed and intolerance that have dictated history thus far. The alternative is untold misery and eventual extinction.'

'How do you fit into all this?'

'First things first,' she said. 'Colin must be spared and allowed to pursue his life without harassment. You promised him as much very recently, but it was only a ruse to get to me. This time, there must be no strings attached.

'He knows too much,' Anderson said flatly.

She smiled coldly. 'You both do.'

'Sorry?'

'I can see what lies beyond the wall you've built in your mind: the change of heart, the broken promise and the crushing guilt that haunts you still.'

Anderson took a deep breath and folded his arms.

Colin had no idea what Wendy was referring to, but it was the first time he'd seen his composure crumble.

'The information you hide can be tapped and sown in other minds. I imagine the personal repercussions would be, at best, unpleasant and, at worst, disastrous.'

Anderson's jaw tightened.

What's she got on him?

Wendy continued: 'Colin isn't a threat. The game has changed beyond all recognition, and you and your masters are powerless to influence its outcome.'

Anderson turned towards him.

Colin shrugged his shoulders. 'Who on earth would believe me anyway?'

Anderson frowned. 'Who indeed?'

Wendy approached Colin and took his hand. 'It's time.'

The Lyrans parted, and she led him down to the water's edge.

She gazed out to sea.

He squeezed her hand. 'What happened to you in the base?'

'The tests they subjected me to acted like switches in my brain. My psychic abilities were boosted, and I suddenly found I could move objects by thought alone.'

'I dreamt about you.'

'I know – I made the dreams. I'm sorry if I frightened you, but I was desperate. That's when the Lyrans picked up my thought patterns and began to communicate with me directly.'

He reached out and eased the electrodes from her head. 'You didn't answer his question.' He tossed them onto the sand. 'How *do* you fit in to all this?'

'I'm part human, part Lyran and part something unique that arose from the union. I can see things clearly now from both perspectives. I'll be the envoy of ʔrts for the changes to come. I'm easier on the eye and ʔe empathic to the nuances of human behaviour.'

ʔnew messiah.'

ʔniled. 'Not quite, but you're on the right lines. ʔal wave was a disaster, and the accident at

292

the Thirlmere base a serious setback, but they adapted their plans accordingly. Dad's gene splicing breakthrough wasn't his own work: the Lyrans guided him all the way. My very existence and destiny were predetermined. They play with a loaded dice because they see things in those time-warped dimensions we can't: chance and opportunity, cause and effect, stretching into a malleable future within which I must play my part.'

'But you said it wouldn't happen for some time.'

'It won't, but my lifespan will be extended accordingly. Don't ask me how because it hasn't been explained to me.'

He ran his fingers through his hair. 'Jesus H ... '

A commotion in the sea stopped their conversation.

About twenty yards out, the water churned and foamed, and a much larger Lyran broke the surface.

'I have to go, Colin.'

'No way! No fucking way!'

'Don't worry; I won't come to any harm.'

Colin looked into the eye of the waiting Lyran. 'Underwater?'

'Only for a short while.'

'What do you mean?'

'Some years ago, these terrestrial Lyrans established contact across interstellar distances by something they term *cerebral net quantum entanglement*. I can't say I really understand it. Apparently, it's a way of bypassing the limitations imposed by the speed of light; a sort of instantaneous communication based on the states of fundamental particles, which they control with their minds. Consequently, a craft has arrived to take me from here and prepare me for the intervention.'

He opened his mouth, but the tumbling words evaporated when she slipped out of the gown and stood naked before him.

The breath caught in his throat as he took her in.

Her breasts were firmer and her body much more toned than he'd imagined in his tender fantasies. The large yellow-tinged bruises on her upper arms and thighs evoked a breath-taking mix of anger and tenderness. He wanted her more than ever. Here and now, on this barren Hebridean beach, surrounded by a surreal ensemble of alien mutations and a disgruntled civil servant.

She moved closer, put her hands on his shoulders and kissed him full on the mouth.

He pulled her to him, but she resisted.

'I want you too, Colin, but it can't be.'

'I won't let you go, Wendy.'

She eased his hands from her arms. 'You have no choice.'

She looked into his eyes with the most penetrating stare he'd ever experienced, and he heard her voice in his mind again.

Eric was right when he said there's something more than our flesh and blood existence. This isn't the end, Colin. I'll share your dreams, and we will meet again many years from now.

I'll hold you to that.

She smiled for the last time. *See that Toby goes to a ~ood home.*

He nodded, and the tears streamed down his cheeks.

e backed away and walked into the sea.

was waist deep when she reached the Lyran and
und. It wrapped her like a cocoon in a gentle
thick, glistening tentacles. The end of one

of them morphed into what looked like a breathing mask over her face. They drifted away until they were around fifty yards from shore and sank slowly into the waves.

A brief, milky glow followed in their wake.

The other Lyrans marched past, heads rising and falling in time with the graceful thrust and sway of their limbs, and swam out to sea.

When the last one submerged, he stared at the flushed clouds on the horizon and wiped away the tears.

Chapter Sixty-six

Anderson appeared at his side.

'Words don't normally fail me,' he said. 'But this is an exception.'

Colin blinked away the remaining tears. 'There isn't anything to say, is there?'

'Nothing that would do it justice.'

They stared out to sea in silence.

Colin glanced at him. 'What did Wendy see in your mind?'

A few moments passed before he replied.

'The sins of my father.'

'Sorry?'

'In the safe house, you asked if the Americans had exposed the person who warned Ms Cooper's father.' He turned to Colin and gave him an unusually warm smile. 'Well, now you know.'

Colin narrowed his eyes. '*Your* father?'

Anderson nodded. 'Recruitment in my profession necessitates a fair amount of nepotism engendered by a time-honoured process of indoctrination that begins around puberty. Consequently, sons, and occasionally daughters, if deemed suitable, often pursue a parent into the most secret of the secret services. Mine was Her Majesty's sole representative at the US base, where he got to know Ms Cooper's father very well. He fully supported his decision to blow the whistle, and, when that failed, he helped him destroy the base and facilitate new identities. He passed the baton to me before he went to a tragically early grave, and I accepted it gladly. But, as the years went by, my opinions changed dramatically. I secretly cursed him for what he had done and vowed to undo it, but the guilt of that betrayal has been a constant thorn in my side. What happened here today, Mr Thurcroft, however extraordinary and unforeseen, is both closure for him and the end of a long and tortuous road for me.'

'If your father helped them escape, how did you lose track of Wendy?'

'They were supposed to start a new life in Peru and maintain twice-yearly contact with my father. Alas, *her* father reneged on his word, and they disappeared into thin air soon after they arrived in Arequipa.'

'Did you mean what you said about using Wendy to eradicate disease and increase life span?'

'Yes, I did. But the possibility of misuse was always there. I was of the opinion that the benefits outweighed the risks, but guarantees are meagre when the stakes are so high. Ultimately, I have to concede that the end result mightn't have been too different from Jeprell's grand plan.'

Colin frowned. 'What happens now?'

He shrugged. 'I shall supervise the destruction of the base, tie up the loose ends, and then submit a full report and my letter of resignation.'

'Really?'

'When you lose the desire to do this job, you become a liability – I will be generously rewarded for my silence and monitored for the rest of my life.'

'And me?'

'Don't worry. I shall redact you from recent events and call in some long overdue favours to keep you out of the limelight.'

'Thanks … '

'Head south along the coast for a couple of miles, and you will come to a shallow bay. You can make your way inland from there.'

Colin nodded and forced a smile. 'Sounds like a plan.'

Anderson checked his watch. 'I ought to be going, and so should you.' He held out his hand, and they shook briefly. 'Goodbye, Mr Thurcroft, and good luck.'

'Same to you … '

Anderson strode towards the cave.

When he disappeared into the darkness, Colin picked up the surgical gown, folded it neatly and slipped it into his inside pocket.

After a last lingering look at the spot where Wendy and the Lyran had submerged, he walked away along the shore. But he didn't get far. A deadening weariness welled up inside him, the sand seemed to drag at his heels, and the rucksack felt like a lead weight on his back.

He sat down and stared at a clump of bedraggled seaweed at his feet.

The stark reality of what had happened was sinking in, and it was hard to deal with. What he'd just witnessed and Wendy's apocalyptic revelation had brought him to the edge of reason. But, at this moment, his main concern was far more personal. He'd been so close to telling her that he loved her, and something had stopped him. He'd fallen head over heels for the old Wendy, but this new incarnation had tempered his emotions with uncertainty and an instinctive fear of the unknown. Could you love somebody who wasn't fully human? Somebody who could read your thoughts, maybe even see the future …

After a couple of minutes, the acrid smell of burning plastic brought him back to the beach. He looked up and saw the bell tower wreathed in black smoke. Dark, wispy tendrils crept towards him from the cave entrance.

He got to his feet, but, as he turned to go, he noticed something out at sea.

It was a small boat, about three hundred yards from shore, heading north.

He shielded his eyes and squinted into the low sun.

Maurie?

A rush of guilt swept through him when he realised he hadn't even mentioned him to Anderson, let alone made a plea for his release.

He slipped off his rucksack and pulled out the binoculars.

There was no doubt it was Candice with Maurie alone at the wheel.

Thank God!

The weariness fell away as he jogged back to where he first came ashore and began to retrace his steps over the slippery seaweed. When he was half way across, he stopped on a large, flat rock and waved his arms. His felt his spirits lift when the boat veered towards him.

By the time he reached the rock ledge, Candice was ten yards away.

The water was at least a foot lower now, and he felt confident about jumping across if Maurie could get near enough. No hesitating this time.

Candice turned side on and bobbed towards him.

'Throw us your rucksack!' Maurie shouted.

Colin tossed the rucksack onto the deck.

He waited for the swell to bring the boat closer, and then leapt over the gunwale.

He slipped on the wet planks, but Maurie caught him by the arm.

'Thanks, mate,' Colin said. 'Superhero to the rescue.'

Maurie gunned the engine, and the boat lurched forward. 'Is it a bird? Is it a plane? No, it's an ageing coke head in his fifty-year-old cabin cruiser.'

Colin laughed. 'You're still a superhero to me.'

Maurie winked. 'All in a day's work, citizen.'

Do I say I saw him hauled away? Maybe not ...

He took the seat across from Maurie.

'Where've you been?' he said. 'I thought you'd have headed home.'

'If only,' Maurie said. 'Just after I dropped you off, fuckin' boat load of marines turn up and start waving guns about. They dragged me off to a holding pen further down the coast. I took the fifth until they found my stash and threatened to arrest me for drug smuggling. I don't know if they swallowed my solo pleasure cruise yarn, but they let me go with the promise of a long stretch if I didn't keep schtum about what I'd seen.' He gestured towards the smoking cliff top. 'And here I am; in one piece but minus a good ounce of the purest Bolivian marching powder this side of the Andes. Hope it chokes the cunts.'

Colin grinned. 'You got off lightly.'

'Oh, you think so?'

He nodded.

'What's *your* story?' Maurie said. 'I take it you didn't find your friend.'

'I did, actually, but there was an unavoidable parting of ways.'

'Is she okay?'

Colin looked out to sea. 'Yeah ... she'll be fine.'

'I would ask more, but I very much doubt you'll tell me.'

He flashed a wry smile. 'I very much doubt you'd believe me, Maurie.'

Chapter Sixty-seven

That night, back at the cottage, they dined on grilled Spam sandwiches, baked beans and Pringles, washed down with various malt whiskies and a couple of white lines for Maurie.

Under a volley of increasingly frank questions, Colin related an improvised and imaginative account of the day's events. He weaved truth, ambiguity and outright lies, with varying success until Maurie's eyes began to close and his empty glass dropped onto the rug.

Both men went to their beds a little after eleven o'clock.

Colin plonked onto the bed, fully-clothed, and sank into a deep sleep.

He had one vivid dream.

He was standing on the beach below the cottage. The cold light of a full moon tinted the wet sand with a gossamer sheen and glinted on the gently lapping waves.

He gazed out to sea in expectation.

On the sharp, cloudless horizon, a pinprick of grey light ignited into a blue glow and rose vertically into the darkness. It raced towards the beach, growing in size and intensity, until it stopped abruptly about twenty feet above him, filling the cool night air with a low, resonant hum.

He stared at the pulsing sapphire sphere, and a feeling of unbridled elation washed through him. It was an order of magnitude more intense than any orgasm, but it wasn't a sexual sensation; it was something more than that, something beyond the physical.

When the humming increased in pitch, he realised he'd lost all sense of time. He could've been there a few seconds or a few hours; it was impossible to say.

But the trance was broken.

A few moments later, the sphere shot upwards at an unimaginable speed.

In less than a second, it was gone.

The moon's scratched and pockmarked visage regarded him with the weary disdain of unimaginable time: an all-too-mortal sack of flesh and bone, as insignificant as the grains of sand he stood upon. And that's exactly how he felt. But it didn't matter anymore. He had no idea why, but he knew, with absolute certainty, that it didn't.

He grinned all the way back to the cottage.

He awoke with a start and glanced at his watch. It was nearly ten past ten.

The hangover wasn't as bad as expected, but his tongue was a slug caught in glue and his stomach fizzed with acidic malcontent.

From the dark edge of memory, the dream teased him with hazy images of a moonlit beach and a bright star. Something had happened there, something moving, life-changing even, but it refused to show itself however much he tried.

Sod it!

He got to his feet and ran his fingers through his hair.

In the kitchen, Maurie was slouched over the table, barefoot, in floral boxer shorts and a crumpled white T-shirt, nursing a steaming mug.

He looked up and raised a listless eyebrow. 'Sleep well?'

Colin yawned. 'Yeah, not bad, thanks.'

Maurie rubbed his temple. 'Must've been off my fuckin' gourd last night. I'm still filling in the blanks.'

Colin smiled. 'It was a long day – I think we both had a bit too much.'

'Did either of us go outside last night?'

He shook his head. 'Don't remember that.'

'To the beach, by any chance?'

'Definitely not,' Colin said. 'Why do you ask?'

'When I got up, the back door was open and there was sand on the floor.'

The dream rushed into his mind.

He quashed the grin as best he could. 'Really?'

'Nothing's missing or out of place, so I can only assume it was one of us.'

He shrugged. 'If I have a flashback, I'll let you know.'

Maurie nodded. 'Same here.' He rose from the chair with some effort and shuffled towards the lounge. 'Help yourself to breakfast – there's bacon and eggs in the fridge, coffee in the pot – you know the score.'

Colin walked over to the toaster, slid the last two slices of bread from the limp plastic bag and dropped them in. He stabbed the lever and gazed out of the kitchen window, across the tangled grass and lumpy dunes, to the slab of grey sea under a storm-raked sky.

The toast burned before he stopped smiling.

Chapter Sixty-eight

Eight days later

Toby jumped onto the couch and snuggled up to Colin.

'Christ's sake,' Jan said. 'Keep him off the furniture.'

'He just needs time to bond with us, Jan. Then you can teach him the house rules.'

'Looks like he's already bonded with *you*.'

'You're only jealous.'

She snorted and grabbed the TV remote. 'Puzzled more like.'

'What do you mean?'

'It's not like you to pick up strays.'

'I married you, didn't I?'

'Ha bloody ha.'

'I almost ran over him. He must belong to somebody, but it was the middle of nowhere, and there wasn't a soul around.'

'That has to be the *third* time you've told me.'

He shrugged and winked at Toby.

Jan continued to channel surf. 'You're not even that keen on dogs.'

'I know, but I like this one, and so does Holly.'

'Why did you call him Toby?'

'Don't know, to be honest – I thought it suited him.'

He stroked Toby's head and recalled the first time he'd met Wendy on the coastal path. The emotions were still raw, and he clenched his teeth to contain them.

It was a couple of minutes before he spoke again.

'By the way,' he said. 'I have to nip to the shop in the morning.'

'On Sunday?'

'Pete's texted a list of stuff he wants me to have a look at, so I thought I'd do it when he's not perched on my shoulder.'

'Just get back in time to make the gravy.'

'Will do.'

Sunday

Colin stood up when the queasiness reached a tolerable level.

He glanced down at his motionless body, and then went to the window.

The weather was very different from his last visit: ochre-tinged storm clouds brooded in an ashen sky, and frail sunlight glistened on wet slate roofs. Only a handful of women, in dark coats and head scarves, scuttled up and down Endell Street. The car had gone from the rear yard, and a dark green tarpaulin draped the Triumph Bonneville.

He waited patiently for nearly half an hour, but Eric didn't show.

As it started to rain, he returned to the armchair and closed his eyes.

When he opened them, bright sunlight was streaming into the room.

He switched off the helmet and got to his feet to walk off the pins and needles.

In the hallway, he closed the door but didn't lock it. He tore a small hole in the handwritten note and eased it over the handle.

He read it one last time.

Pete,
You can empty this room now.
Throw the furniture in the skip.
Cheers,
Colin

He lingered there for a few moments, and then turned and walked away.

Epilogue

Joyce Manning got up from her armchair and froze when the pain hit.

She clutched her chest and slumped back down.

She took a few laboured breaths, but it didn't do any good.

The pain spread to her back, and beads of cold sweat broke out on her forehead.

She closed her eyes and gritted her teeth.

It was agony now and getting steadily worse.

She gripped the arms of the chair and let out a silent scream as the unbearable pressure threatened to burst through her ribcage.

Then, in an instant, it was gone.

An intense euphoria washed through her.

She opened her eyes and saw her brother standing over her.

He held out his hands, and she took them and rose with an ease she hadn't felt for fifty years or more.

He looked into her eyes and smiled as the room melted away and an intense, pure white light lit them from above.

The End

Lightning Source UK Ltd.
Milton Keynes UK
UKOW05f0038311214

243811UK00005B/592/P